CW00301303

THE
DAMNED
ONES

Published by Dark Titan Publishing. A subsidiary of Dark Titan Imaginations and Products. A division of The Dark Titan Company.

Hardcover ISBN: 979-8-9886918-2-2
Paperback ISBN: 979-8-9886918-0-8
eBook ISBN: 979-8-9886918-1-5

darktitanpublishing.com

EverWar UNIVERSE
THE DAMNED ONES

TY'RON W. C. ROBINSON II

DARK TITAN PUBLISHING

THE STORY OF

BOC - BATTLE OF CAELUM
AOC - AFTER BATTLE OF CAELUM

CONTENTS

"SHADOWED IN THE DARKNESS OF THE STELLARSPACE, PROPHECY FORTELLS THE DEAD'S RETURN." - TENET OF MORS

CHAPTER 1

REVENGE OF THE VIPER LORDS

Ships swarmed over the skies of the planet Ro. Volcanoes across the land, erupting at every corner of the seconds in which were passing. The ships in the air blasting toward each other. The Revolter Squadron and Eglah Aeronauts. Beams of lightning flashed throughout the smoky sky. On the grounds of Ro was a battle of its own. Four Aduroblades colliding with the bolting sounds of thunder emulating. Shockwaves quickening the rocks below. Two forces stood in the fight. A blast of energy shoves one away from the other.

"Did you think you could just escape us?" Sinth Cain asked.

"I wasn't trying to escape." Aweran Serkelrod answered. "I was only giving time it's needed favor."

The Knight of the Covenant clashed his Aduroblades once more as Sinth Cain blocked the coming strike with his own. The brightening color of Aweran's aduroblade struck in the light of Cain's darkening aduroblade. On the other side of the desolated landscape were Zeena Lyh and Sinth Kara. The two women continued their battle with ferocity in their attacks. Zeena was on the defensive while Kara remained steadfast in the offence. Such was her nature as she is a Viper Lord.

The battle in the air continued with the Ark-Fighters and Eglahs in a dogfight of their own. A war consumed the planet of Ro. Not much different than the previous battle on the planet of Thran. Six decades have passed since the incident. The Knights of the Covenant retreated into a form of peace after their victory. Unknown to them at least, Sinth Cain and Sinth Kara had devised a plan to summon the Knights from their peaceful lives and to bring them back into conflict. The Knights were not fools to be made of. They knew what the Viper Order was planning and what they desired. They wanted another battle. Another war.

Sinth Cain raised his right hand as dark flames consumed it. The ground shook with Aweran believing it to been caused by the erupting volcanoes, yet, from the growing cracks in the ground, demons arose. Small imps in nature. Their eyes glowing like the lava surrounding them. Their bodies skin cracked and boiling, pulsing with fluids. Almost as if they've originated from the planet's core.

"I figured I could use some assistance." Cain scoffed.

"Your powers are beyond darkness." Aweran said. "The Dekar has ruined you. You and your wife."

"The Dekar has proven me a great service. You and your kind should've adopted it sooner. Otherwise, you would be on the winning side."

"There is only one winning side. That is all of the Avior."

Aweran paced his steps and rushed into battle with a swift strike toward the snarling demons. The aduroblade slashing through the demons with ease, moving them out of his path. The touch of the blade evaporated the demons, breaking them down into small pebbles before they evaporated into the air. Cain was impressed, reaching to his right side and pulling out the Sinthblade.

"You've bested me before in such a manner." Cain said, holding the Sinthblade and his aduroblade. "Let's see how much you've learned since then."

Cain struck with his aduroblade first with Aweran deflecting the attack before seeing the Sinthblade rise above him. The blades clashed with the rolling thunder, blasting hem away from one another. Elsewhere, Zeena and Kara continued their fight with Zeena's adurostaff blocking most of Kara's rushed and angry strikes. Kara did not stop with her attacks. One after the other, pushing Zeena back, closer to a thriving lavafall. Kara screamed as she slammed her aduroblade into Zeena's staff, shoving her toward the pouring lava overhead. Zeena held her own against the angry Viper Lord as Kara continued to scream in her anger.

"Just die!"

"No."

Above them was an Eglah. The winged orb craft flew in the distance as it is was quickly shot down by an incoming Ark-Fighter. The Eglah crashed upon the ground behind Kara, blasting her and Zeena toward the lavafall. Zeena grabbed the air in her palms and pressed forward, blasting her and Kara back toward the crashed ship and away from the lavafall. Kara laid on the ground as her hood was removed and her cloak burned from the crash debris. She turned her gaze to see the downed eglah and the aeronaut screaming as he climbed out of the burning ship before falling to his death. Kara looked forward, seeing Zeena standing, catching her breath.

"I'm already down." Kara said. "Go ahead, finish the job."

"There's no honor in killing you while you're down." Zeena said, holding her adurostaff. "Get up. Fight me with honor."

Kara scoffed with a hint of a giggle as she stood up. Holding her aduroblade steady as it began to exhort a stronger force of energy. Wiping he blood from her mouth and the sweat from her forehead. She glared at Zeena with even more hatred.

"Honor. Such is the nature of those who will never see the true path."

"The true path is in honor. Only you have forsaken it."

Kara began to fume as she went back to attacking Zeena. Swinging her aduroblade in every corner of his sight. Zeena backed up from the strikes, deflecting a few of them before twirling the staff, hitting Kara's abdomen. The Viper Lord paused in her attack as she glanced down, seeing herself bleeding. She scoffed slowly.

"So this is how I fall. In battle against one of the Avior?"

"It seems so."

"Finish it." Kara said.

Zeena nodded and with one more slash, the adurostaff collided into Kara shoulder and exited through her side. Her body split as it fell to the ground. Sinth Kara is dead. Zeena looked around as she could hear the battle between Aweran and Cain ongoing. She ran to reach them. The two continued their battle, both losing their step and nearly out of breath. Aweran pushed the air against Cain, blowing him backwards as he tripped from the impact. Cain rose up as Zeena arrived in their viewpoint.

"Aweran!" Zeena yelled.

"Zeena!"

Cain looked around as he was preparing for another strike. While doing such, he paused just as Zeena entered the battlefield. He was confused. He stopped and began looking around. Almost frantically.

"Where is she?" Cain asked. "Where is she?"

"She's dead." Zeena said. "She died in battle. With honor."

Cain was frozen. His aduroblade fell to the ground. Shaking his head in disbelief. He couldn't imagine Kara to have been killed. His eyes turned from their natural red to a much darker red. The winds around them began to pick up as he held the Sinthblade with both hands. His eyes locked in on the two Knights.

"Get behind me." Aweran said, holding his aduroblade tightly.

"You took her from me. From me!"

Cain screamed with pure anger, rushing toward them with the Sinthblade. Aweran did not move and with a quick strike, Cain stopped and fell to the ground. Aweran raised up his aduroblade, covered in blood. One quick slash from the blade had killed Cain.

"It is over." Zeena said.

"It is. Finally."

The battle in the air came to an abrupt end as the aeronauts received word of the Viper Lords' demise. Retreating to the stars, the Ark-Fighter pilots celebrated their victory. Aweran and Zeena returned to their Helio Sor ship to give out the news to their allies: The Lords of the Viper are dead and the Knights of the Covenant remain supreme.

CHAPTER II

THE LOVE OF TWO

Having returned to their home city of Tropolton, the largest city in all of the planet Helio, the Knights celebrated their victory against he Viper Order back on Ro. Aweran was mostly celebrated for his achievement in defeating Sinth Cain as was Zeena in her battle with Sinth Kara. The Knights came forward in the open room. Amzi Grake, Ebed El-Ezer, Novad Tengu, and Orvan Shackleford. Hugs spread through the room. Once the celebration had ended, Aweran and Zeena went onto the balcony of the Tropolton palace, overlooking the vast wilderness which sat before them as the moonlight scattered across the grounds of Helio.

"Now that the Viper Lords are dead, what do we do next?" Zeena asked.

"Time will tell. There will always be another battle. Another war. This life is fated for it."

"But what about us?"

"What about us?"

"Us. You and me. We're already married. Eventually, we'll have to raise a family of our own."

"I know. But now isn't exactly the time. Wars are calling. No need to put anyone in danger."

"No one's in danger." Zeena said, approaching Aweran closely. "The High One watches over all of us."

"Strangely enough, I once thought you didn't believe in such things early on."

"I did. I just never showed it."

While the two went in for a kiss, an Elder Knight stood behind, calling for their attention. They saw him and quickly reverted to their duteous roles, bowing before his presence.

"Elder Knight." The two said.

"I do not wish to intrude on such an occasion. But, Aweran, I must have a word with you."

Zeena smiled as she held Aweran's hand. Letting it go as she walked away. The Elder Knight took notice as he approached the balcony, standing beside Aweran.

"I know this might seem strange, but-"

"There's nothing strange about it, Aweran. You two are married. Only most of the Knights never show affection unless their inside their chambers. A way to keep the outsiders out of one's affairs."

"Thank you, grandfather."

"I heard enough of your conversation. Zeena is right. One day, your son must follow in your footsteps. A Knight of the Covenant he will become."

"How can I be a father when most of the Stellarspace needs our support?"

"I'll give you an example. Your father Laban married your mother in a time of such warfare. Through the battles, she gave birth to you when your father was on other planets, doing the work of a Knight of the Covenant."

"That's what he always told me when he came around. I'm doing the same aren't I?"

"Indeed, you truly are your father's son. As was he my own."

"I am wondering what's next for us? The Viper Lords are dead. Surely other nations will hear of the news. Seeking a way to start another conflict."

"There are many conflicts throughout the Stellarspace. Only to make sure you choose the right one for the right cause."

"I guess we'll find out."

"One more thing, I heard about what happened on the battlefield back on Thran. You came in contact with something strange?"

"Yes. Something spoke to me during my battle with Sinth Cain.

Urging me to give in to the Dekar. To use it against Cain."

The Elder Knight sighed. Rubbing his beard.

"I knew this would come again once more."

"What would?"

"It's part of our lineage. A majority of the Knights are aware of our ancestors. Going back several generations. A curse was made of our family line. Stating some of us will be intertwined with the Avior and the Dekar. A mixture that could only bring about damnation."

"I'm guessing this occurred during the ancient wars."

"The Cavalier Civil War in particular. Nearly during the War of Helio with Grandfather Yabel, but he managed to overcome the temptation. His grandson however did not."

"I see."

"This is why I must warn you. If you ever come across the strange spirit once again, turn away from it. Mute out its words, for the will do anything to slip into your ears and consume your mind. The Dekar is not something you wish to have. No matter how powerful it makes those who have it appear."

"It did seem powerful when the Viper Lords were using it against us. Zeena told me Sinth Kara used it to summon demons."

"I have seen it myself. The Dekar is fully consumed into darkness. That is why we must trust in The High One and the Avior He has gifted to us."

Aweran nodded in his understanding. The Elder Knight noticed it and allowed him to return to Zeena.

Elsewhere, on the planet Moraltis, sadness filled the land as the Sinth-Tred ship returned from Ro with the bodies of Sinth Cain and Sinth Kara inside. Their bodies and weapons were brought into the throne room to the presence of the Chief Cardinals. Their blood-red robes could catch the eyes of anyone. Even their headdresses were even an impressive style. They saw their bodies and bowed their heads.

"Our leaders are dead. Gone into the ether of The Fallen One."

"We know what must be done." The second Cardinal said.

"Yes. We wait for the Supreme Cardinal to make the decision. Afterwards, we shall continue on with our plans."

From the doors came forth the Supreme Cardinal. His long white robes outshined the other Cardinals. A face very grim, anyone could tell he was a Moraltian. He approached the bodies of Cain and Kara. He sighed bitterly. Looking at their weapons, he reached for the Sinthblade and held it in his hands.

"Bury them with their blades."

Behind him approached two Imperial Viper Knights. Cloaked and robed like the Cardinals. They each held a side of the pad the Viper Lord bodies laid and took it from the throne room.

"My Supreme," One of the Cardinals said. "What must we do now?"

"Summon Bishop Obliteran and Lady Ivah to this room. Tell them it's time."

"Yes, my Supreme."

The two Cardinals went ahead and brought Bishop Obliteran and Lady Ivah into the throne room, where they stood before the Supreme Cardinal. The Cardinals showed their obeisance toward them, even the Supreme Cardinal. For the ranks of Obliteran and Ivah were much higher than theirs.

"You summoned us, Supreme Cardinal?" Obilteran asked.

"I did. You are the first to know of the deaths of Sinth Cain and Sinth Kara. As of this moment, the Viper Lords are dead and are now reborn. With the two of you. Prepare yourselves for the Ceremony of the Dekar in three hours' time."

They listened to the Cardinal's words and prepared themselves separate in the preparation rooms. Aided by servants, they removed their previous garments and put on the new ones. Dark-clad attire. Small touches of fire-red stitched into them. Both had cloaks and hoods. Once the five hours had passed, Obilteran and Ivah entered the ceremony room together to the sight of a large crowd. A similar sight to all the events which took place in the ceremony room. The rainshockers, howlshockers, Imperial Viper Knights, and the residents all bow their heads toward

Obilteran and Ivah, paying respect and honor to them and their new rank. Obilteran and Ivah approached the podium where the Supreme Cardinal stood. He blessed them and handed them both their own aduroblades. When they pulled them from their sheaths, the surrounding area brightened like a red sky. Ivah's blade shined with a pure red. Red as rubies. But Obliteran's blade was shrouded with a darkened hue of red. A bleeding shine. The smiles upon their faces grew wider at the sight of such weaponry as they were only skilled primarily in standard swords and daggers.

"There is one more." The Cardinal said, raising up the Sinthblade. "This weapon, one that has been passed down through the generations of all Viper Lords that have come before you. This day, you are now its new bearer. Wield the Sinthblade, the Blade of the Dekar with great power and no mercy."

The Cardinal handed the Sinthblade to Obliteran. He looked upon it, mesmerized by the ancient writing upon the sheath and the markings left behind by the previous wielders.

"Do the two of you agree to stand side by side in all your works for the glory of the Dekar?" The Cardinal asked.

"We do." Obliteran and Ivah said.

"Man, do you agree to give the proper orders and instructions to those below your rank and make sure they excel in their works given to them in the glory of the Dekar?"

"I do."

"Woman, do you agree to stand by your husband and obey all that he has to speak toward you and your works?"

"I do."

"Man, do you swear upon the Lord of the Dekar that you will remain faithful to him, to the Viper Order, and to your wife?"

"I do."

"Woman, do you swear to love your husband above all the things within the realm we live in and serve him until your time of calling is at hand?"

"I do."

"Now, the both of you, join arms."

Obliteran and Ivah joined arms. Obliteran's left arm to the Ivah's right. Within the middle of them stood the Sinthblade, which Obliteran held in his left hand. The Cardinal stood tall as he commanded them to raise their joined arms above their heads and so they did.

"This day, I, Supreme Cardinal Zedka, by the laws written in *The Moraltic Bible*, I proclaim the two of you to be henceforth known as Sinth Obliteran and Sinth Ivah. This day forward, the two of you are now crowned, the new Viper Lords of the Order and new members of Those of the Dekar!"

The crowd cheered on their new rulers of Moraltis with a great thunder of applause.

"Then it is settled for all of Moraltis to witness and to know." The Cardinal said toward the crowd, facing them with great stature. "I give to you this day, Sinth Obliteran and Sinth Ivah! Applaud your new Viper Lords! Give great shouts toward The Fallen One. Praise the Dekar with all your might!"

Obliteran turned to Ivah and the two shared a kiss as he took the Sinthblade out of its sheath, sensing its great energy emitting from deep within the blade. Obilteran grinned and held it high above him to a great applause and cheers. New Viper Lords were made and Those of the Dekar continue on.

"Lastly," Supreme Cardinal Zedka said to the new Lords. "let the power of the Dekar surge through your being. Let its power show you true knowledge and understanding. With it, the two of you will be able to do and accomplish anything of your heart's desires."

A great feast was held in their honor as many of the residents of the planet came to visit them. Granting them with gifts and offerings of their servitude. The two new Viper Lords consummated their new positions and rulership inside their new chambers to please one another. To fully become one flesh and one of the Dekar.

Meanwhile, back in Tropolton, Aweran and Zeena spent some time together themselves.

CHAPTER III

SIGNS OF THE FUTURE

In the sky was dark and covered in smoke. Embers of white flames floated above like fireflies. Crashed Ark-Fighters and Eglahs down in the dirt. The robes of the Ordowian sorcerers laid flat on the ground, some burnt from the fires. Even traits of the Sinstorian armies were deep in the dirt. Their weapons broken in pieces. Across from them were bodies of rain shockers. Their chests darkened from a strong attack for their armor was covered in burn marks. Zeena was fighting for her life on a desolated battlefield against a cloaked figure. Face shrouded from the light. The figure was double her size and its strength outnumbered her. She went for a strike with her adurostaff, only for the figure to deflect the coming blow and impale her with its own blade. Zeena stood frozen as the figure shoved her off its blade. As her body fell to the ground came six more figures, cloaked in darkness behind the large one. They stood and oversaw the destruction around them. The large one's eyes shined with a pure whiteness. In its eyes was nothing. They were dead.

Aweran jolted from his sleep in the night, shaking himself as he was sweating. Beside him, Zeena was awoken to the sound of Aweran's stuttering speech. She reached over to his arm, holding him.

"What is it?"

"Something's strange. Something's wrong."

"You can share it with me."

Aweran looked into Zeena's eyes and slowly shook his head. Holding back tears. Aweran gets up from the bed, dressing himself. Zeena remained on the bed, confusion covered her face.

"Where are you going?"

"I need to speak with Grandfather. I think he can help me with… this."

"With what? A nightmare."

"I think it's more than a nightmare."

Aweran left his chambers and paced himself down the corridors, approaching his grandfather's study. Opening the door slightly, he looked inside to find his grandfather sitting at his desk, researching various maps. awe ran knocked to grab his attention as his grandfather looked up with ease.

"I'm sorry to disturb you so late."

"You would only do so if there was something important to share."

"It is." Aweran said, walking toward the desk. "I had a dream. A nightmare."

"Nightmare? What of a sort?"

"I saw a land desolated. Revolter ships and Viper Order eglahs crashing from the sky. Flames were white as a blinding light. I saw rainshockers, sorcerers, Ard-Knights, even the Elves, dead."

"I'm sensing there's something else."

"I saw Zeena, fighting some strange entity. It was shadowed in black. Completely from head to toe. He killed her. After he did, six other shadowed ones appeared behind him. His eyes, they had no life in them."

"Did you get a look at their uniforms?"

"They… they looked like Emerald Cavaliers. Only in black."

The Elder Knight raised up in his chair. His eyes focused on Aweran's words. Aweran could only stare as his grandfather said nothing. It caused a concern to Aweran. The silence of his grandfather continued. Almost as if fear itself entered the room.

"Grandfather?" Aweran said.

"Don't mind me, we need to speak with someone of a higher rank. He'll know for certain what your dream entails."

The Elder Knight stood up from his desk as Aweran followed him out of the stud and down the other corridors. They walked without saying a word. The Elder Knight moved with as much haste if not more than his grandson. They reached a room near the very end of one of the corridors.

The door was surrounded with the energy of the Avior. Stronger than anything Aweran's encountered. The Elder Knight was aware of the energy, bowing his head.

"Who's in there?" Aweran asked.

"One of the greatest Elder Knights to have ever exist."

The Elder Knight knocked. A voice echoed from the inside, permitting them entrance. The Elder Knight opened the door, he and Aweran walked in and their eyes were set on the Elder Knight sitting before them. An old man, cloaked in a white robe. His white hair blended in perfect with his attire. Aweran watched as his grandfather approached him and knelt in his sight. Aweran followed, doing the same.

"Aweran, meet Elder Knight Ocha. One of the Avior and a Prophet of The High One."

Ocha observed them. Setting his eyes closely toward Aweran. His energy in the Avior overpowered theirs and it could be easily felt within the room.

"Elder Knight Jad Serkelrod and Knight Aweran Serkelrod. I know the purpose of your visit."

"You know?" Aweran said. "How?"

"I am more in tune with the Avior than most of the Knights on this planet. There's a many things one can do with such power."

"Elder Knight Ocha," Jad said. "Forgive us for bothering you at such a late time. My grandson must give you the insight to his dream."

"You dreamt of destruction, yes?"

"I did."

"And you saw these shadow beings? You saw our wife fall by their leader's blade?"

"I did. What does it mean?"

"The shadow beings you saw were known in the times of old as the Onyx Cavaliers. A legion of soldiers from the planet Mors. Undead beings corrupted by a much darker magic. Even darker than the Dekar. The one who killed your wife was named Black Hood. Their leader."

"Elder," Jad said. "Does my grandson's dream have a meaning?"

"Yes. Whenever someone dreamt of the Onyx Cavaliers, it was an impending sign of their return. What you saw, young Serkelrod, was a future to come."

"No!" Aweran said.

"Do not fear." Ocha replied. "It is only a future. Not the future."

"Then, we must find a way to divert this future. We must seek out something to protect her from this undead force."

"Your wife is not the only concern here. The Onyx Cavaliers seek to destroy all life in the Stellarspace. From your dream, your wife was on the frontlines for this war. One of the last ones to defend."

"What must be done, Elder?" Jad asked.

"With this dream occurring, I know the Emerald Cavaliers are preparing to strike them when the time arrives. However, I know of an artifact that was once used during the Cavalier Civil War to stop them, trapping them on their planet."

"Where's the artifact now?" Aweran questioned. "Is it in the possession of the Viper Lords or the Magus Court?"

"No. it's on Erets-Alpha. In a small village."

"I'll get myself ready and head on out there."

"Take with you the Knights who you traveled with on your past journey." Ocha said. "It will be a benefit on this quest of yours."

"I will do as you command, Elder Ocha." Aweran said, leaving the room.

Jad watched as his grandson exited. Ocha sighed.

"I sense it in him already.' Ocha said. "The Dekar. It's growing at a sands pace."

"He informed me of a spirit he encountered back on Thran. It tried to compel him to use the Dekar in order to defeat the Viper Lords. He refused. Relied on the Avior for his victory."

"He did well." Ocha nodded. "But, the essence remains."

"He may have a chance. I didn't succumb to the Dekar."

"True. You managed to overcome its temptations. As did we all. Aweran's young. His strength isn't strong enough to full turn away from such power."

"It will take some time. As it did with our forefathers."

"This is true. Keep an eye on him. Make sure he doesn't fall to the Dekar as those who've come before him."

"I will do my best."

Jad nodded as he exited the room. Ocha remained in his seat. His eyes closed as the door closed on its own.

On Moraltis, the new Viper Lords had met inside the strategic room. The room surrounded with commanders and generals. Upon their entrance into the room, the Elite Commander saw them and quickly bowed. The others in the room followed suit. The Viper Lords appreciated their servitude as they walked over to the war table detailed with every known planet throughout the Stellarspace and the sectors they resided in. On the table, Obliteran marked the planet Helio and grunted as he did.

"We must eliminate them. They murdered our predecessors. Left their bodies on a foreign planet with no regard for their souls."

"In all good time." Ivah said. "But they aren't the only ones we need to take out."

Ivah moved another marker, laying it over the planet of Dagobar.

"You wish to take down the orchs?"

"They are a conniving species. Barbarism is all they know. We shall teach them the true meaning of civilization under Moraltian law."

"I agree to that. However, we cannot strike them all at the same time. We do not have enough forces to make such a move."

"We have allies." Ivah said, pointing toward the planets of Sinstor and Ordow.

"The Sinstorians are preoccupied with their ongoing affairs. The Ordowians would only align with us if it benefited them. You know they prefer their magic over the Dekar."

"Like I said. All in good time."

CHAPTER IV

SECTOR ZERO

The cold darkness of Sector Zero. Everything looked as if it stood still. A sector barren of life. Nothing living. Not even the stars, for they were also dead. In the midst of the sector rested a planet. A planet void of color and life. The lands of Mors were dead. For there was no life. No animals. Nothing that could be seen as life. It is said during the ancient days, Mors was a thriving place. Filled with many forests, oceans, and life as many see fit. A kingdom Mors once had with tenets of their own. Many nations across the Stellarspace respected the Morsians for their honor and their culture. Until corruption came upon them and ruined the planet within. Only in the mountain regions of Mors came a loud shout. A battle cry echoed through the valleys. Within those valleys rested an army. Cloaked in the shadows, yet only their eyes could be seen. Pure white eyes. Only dead. The battle cries continued as one larger shadow presented itself atop the mountains, gazing down at the dead army.

"We are prepared!" The shadowed figure screamed. "The signs of the stars have been delivered. We have been in the shadows long enough. Now, it is our time. For the Stellarspace has not seen our kind for many eons. This day, it changes. Rally yourselves, for the God of the Dead is our guide and our judge. The Nations battle each other like animals to their prey. They will not see us coming. This universe is ours. It will belong to the Dead!"

The undead army continued to shout. Their weapons raised above their heads. Dark blades, glistening with the same white as their eyes.

"Your weapons are ready. Sharpened and skilled. As is mine!"

The figure atop the mountain lifted his own weapon. A weapon much larger than the ones below him. His weapon glowed, as it was a pure white light coated on a darkened blade. The armies below let out a short gasp as they saw the glowing nature of his blade.

"I, Black Hood, will lead you all into battle. As it is my fate. As it is yours to see for our victory. For the Dead, we shall fight! For the God of the Dead, we shall worship! In the Undead, we are One!"

The armies screamed with a great shout, rocking the mountains around them with shockwaves. Their leader marched them toward their large ship, known as the *Shamhuth*. The armies were prepared as they took off. The Onyx Cavalier Force had left Mors and entered the vast Stellarspace.

CHAPTER V

THE LAND WHERE ENASH BEGAN

The Knights of the Covenant arrived on Erets-Alpha, coming down into the metropolitan city of Coolts, Aweran's hometown. The city still gleaming with bright lights and tall buildings. Skyscrapers nearly reached the clouds above as many ships covered the skies. Landing their ship in the city port, the residents of the city gazed their eyes upon the Knights, bowing before them. Others recognize Aweran from years prior, eagerly cheering him on.

"Good thing they remember you." Amzi said.

"I thought they would've forgotten. Didn't spend a lot of time around them before then."

"Right now, we should be focused on finding this object Elder Ocha has commanded for us to retrieve."

Knight Orvan reached into his bag, pulling out a map. Upon it were several marked locations. He pointed at them for all the Knights to see. The first one called *Erac* was to the north. Another one, called the *City of Iericho* to the east and the last one, called *Urim* to the south.

"Which one is it?" Knight Novad asked.

"We'll have to search them all." Amzi replied. "We can split up. Search the villages in teams. Gives up enough time to grab and go."

"I agree." Aweran said. "Me and Zeena will search Erac."

"I'll be joining you both." Elder Jad replied. "Three of us make a lighter work. Besides, Erac is a grim city. Settled by Star Raiders, Venators, and the like. It won't be easy getting in or getting out."

Aweran nodded. Agreeing with his grandfather as did Zeena.

"Then we'll be careful." Aweran replied.

"Very well." Amzi said. "Myself and Ebed will go and search Iericho. We're familiar with the old city. The path into the city is right next to one of the old trade routes used for silk."

"Then that leaves me and Orvan for Urim." Novad said. "We'll need some land-vehoes for this search. Gives us a faster pace."

"You two are headed to Urim." Amzi said. "You'll both need desert-vehoes. They travel better on the sands. Land-veho will only slow you down."

Novad nodded.

"I'll take your word for it."

Everyone was ready and they went and acquired their vehicles from the nearby transportation department, a place that frequently rents out many vehicles for tourists of the city and the planet as a whole for Coolts was the mainstay of the entire planet. They rode off through the large city, spreading out as they reached the outskirts of Coolts. Amzi and Ebed went east. Novad and Orvan turned south. Aweran, Zeena, and Jad turned north. Riding through the countrylands, Aweran looked as he they were coming up to his old neighborhood.

"Wait." Aweran said.

"What is it?" Zeena asked.

"I need to see something first."

Zeena and Jad followed Aweran as he rode through the countryman homes, stopping in front of one which appeared to be vacant. Stepping off his veho, Aweran stood in awe as he looked at the home. Zeena approached him from behind, seeing the home.

"Who's here?"

"No one." Aweran said. "This is my home."

Aweran approached the door, reaching into his pocket. He pulled out a key and scoffed. Unlocking the door as if it was still the days prior to his knighthood years. The door had opened and Aweran saw, everything that was there when he left, remained. Everything was untouched. They entered the home as Aweran could only stare in silence. Walking past the counter, the table, and all his old belongings. It felt as if time has a sense of rewinding for the Knight.

"I remember this place." Jad said. "I came here from time to time when your father was alive. You were only an infant in those days."

"This table." Aweran said. "This is where I was when Elder Amzi suggested I come along with them. This is where my life changed."

"Your mother didn't stay here?" Zeena asked.

"She moved to Highorth sometime after my father's death. I stayed with her until I was of age. I returned here. To keep the home in our family."

Aweran sighed as he arose from the table. Knowing they have an artifact to look for, they left the home. Aweran took one last look as he closed the door. The three rode off down the road, exiting the countryside.

Riding eastward, Amzi and Ebed rode into the low terrain, arriving in the Cit of Iericho. A small population as it had always been since its early destruction in the ancient days. Riding through the city, the people knew them to be Knights. Their uniforms were clear enough of an indication. However, the people felt uneasy them in their city. Ebed couldn't understand why. Amzi knew why. History always returns in many forms.

"Rayen." Amzi said softly.

"Rayen?" Ebed said. "Your ancestor?"

"I remember hearing about how he came into this city once during the War for Helio during his early days as a Knight. He came into some minor conflicts here. Ierichons don't take kindly to outsiders. Particularly Knights of the Covenant. It's our fault why this city never returned to its former glory."

"There's always an ancient war to rekindle old flames."

"Such is the life we live."

Their vehoes stopped as they were confronted by an older man and two guards. Amzi and Ebed stepped from their vehoes as they approached the three men, seeing their hands to their sides. Near their swords.

"We bring no trouble." Amzi said. "We're here on important duties."

"Pfft." The old man jolted. "It's always an important duty when it comes to Knights of the Covenant. Don't act like we've forgotten what your kind done to us."

"We were not here during the ancient days. It is not our fight. We bring no conflict."

"Then why are you here?"

"We're here to ask if you are in possession of a peculiar artifact."

"What does this artifact look like?"

Ebed pulled out a device, presenting a holographic image of the artifact. The old man nodded.

"I'm familiar with it. Some kind of staff. Very powerful."

"Do you have it?" Amzi asked.

"Unfortunately no. if I did, I would hand it to you. Just to get you two out of our city."

"We'll be out of here if you know where it was taken?"

"True. True. Last I remember, it was given to the dwellers in the southern regions. As some kind of tool to use in their worship services. I know not where. Only that it was done."

Amzi and Ebed knew where and greeted the three men farewell, leaving Iericho.

Aweran, Zeena, and Jad continued riding north, looking ahead as they passed a sign welcoming them into the regions of Erac. The scenery changed greatly. From the lush countrylands to a now deserted and isolated landscape. Seeing machinery as far as the eye could see. Nothing out there was capable of travel. Neither on land, under the seas, or in the air. Around them, they saw many Star Raiders digging through the stockpiles of minerals. Almost scavenging for parts.

"Keep your guard up." Jad said. "These people aren't the trustworthy kind."

Entering the city of Erac, the smell in the air reminded them of oil. Many Raiders stand outside of the buildings. Talking. Drinking.

Smoking. Aweran and Zeena felt unsettled in their sights. Jad was familiar to the scenery. He wasn't bothered by their stares.

"Let's stop here." Jad said, pointing toward the tavern. "Ask someone about this artifact."

"How would they know?" Zeena wondered.

"Anything that goes through this place, you can count on these kinds of people to know."

They parked vehoes as the Raiders continued to watch them. Jad told Aweran and Zeena not to worry, the Raiders know who they are and wouldn't dare seek conflict with them. Walking into the tavern, the odor of burning metal and ale covered filled the air. Many Raiders, even Venators and Strikefighters were sitting inside. Smoking and drinking is their usual leisure activity. Others played a game of *Horlo*. Jad approached the bartender with a nod.

"I know you and your friends aren't here to drink. You want information."

"Yes. Tell me, are you aware of a strange artifact roaming through the region?"

"Depends on what this artifact looks like."

"A staff. Over six feet in height. Made of a silvery-gold substance. Light to the touch. Very powerful energy within it."

The bartender nodded, inching closer toward Jad.

"I've seen it." The bartender whispered.

"You have? Where can we find it?"

"Head south. It was given to the dwellers down there for safekeeping. They use it during their worship ceremonies. Gives off a powerful light in the night. Everyone from here to Coolts can see it touching the sky."

Jad smiled.

"Thank you for your service." Jad said, passing the bartender some shekels of silver.

Jad returned to Aweran and Zeena. They could tell he had some information by the expression on the bartender's face has he counted the silver pieces.

"You bribed him off, grandfather?"

"I simply paid a good man some fair wages for helping us with an important cause. It is our duty to protect after all."

"Novad and Orvan are on the right course. They'll get to the artifact before we will."

"Might as well travel southward." Zeena said. "Meet them there."

"Agreed." Jad said. "Let's get out of here."

They returned outside to their vehoes, spotting three Raiders looking at them closely. Touching the vehicles as if they were their own. Aweran approached them fast, raising up his aduroblade. The Raiders saw them, quickly drawing out their ranges. Zeena followed Aweran, raising up her adurostaff as did Jad. The air became tense around the tavern.

"Best thing you boys do is back away from our vehoes." Jad said.

"Best listen to him." Aweran said. "Before I cut you down."

"Just like the Knights." One Raider said. "Always with the threats."

"These are threats." Zeena rebutted. "It's a guarantee."

The Raiders were shaking. Their rangers were not even held steady. One of the Raiders began whispering to his friends. They listened and slowly lowered their rangers, stepping aside. Jad nodded as Aweran sheathed his aduroblade.

"You boys did good." Jad said. "Don't make the same mistake again."

"Or what?" The third Raider said.

Jad sighed. Aweran's hand grabbed the hilt as his aduroblade arose once more, slashing away the Raider's range. Splitting it in half. Near his fingers. The Raider let out a shivering yell as he ran away with his friends following.

"That scared them off." Zeena said.

"Yes." Jad replied. "Yes it did. But it was not necessary."

"I'm sorry, grandfather. But we are in a hurry are we not?"

"We are. Let's get out of this forsaken city."

Just as they rode out of Erac, an old friend of theirs arrived on the other end. Moving in a hurry as his duster flowed with the wind, Evad Nod ran into the tavern, starting those inside. He approached the bartender with haste, removing his hat and asking for a drink. The bartender slid him a drink.

"Another chase, Nod?" The bartender asked.

"Something like that."

"Who is it this time?"

"A Venator. One angry Venator."

"Does this angry Venator have a name? Perhaps I know of them?"

"Ever heard of Jakah Pen?"

"The infamous Venator who aided the Viper Order? He's after you?"

"No. His son is."

"Oh." The bartender paused. "Dovan Pen is chasing you? You know he has determination to complete his contracts."

"I know. Still trying to figure out how to get him off my back."

"Maybe those Knights could help you out."

"What Knights?"

"The Covenant Knights. Three of them were in here not too long ago."

"Which ones? What did they look like?"

"Three of them. I know the older one. The other guy must've been a lower-tier Knight as was the woman."

"Aweran. Zeena." Evad spoke quietly under his breath. "Ah, great! Where are they headed?"

"Gong south near Urim. You can try and catch up before they leave the planet."

Evad took a moment to think. He knew them. He drank the rest of his drink and stormed outside, returning to his ship. Just as he took off, Dovan Pen arrived in Erac. His armor was blue as a sapphire, yet shiny as a ruby.

Down southward, Novad and Orvan arrived in Urim. An ancient city-state. One of the very important spiritual activities. The two Knights were quickly greeted by the residents of the area. They were dressed in the fashion of the ancients. They lived in tents made of the hides of great beasts. Even their weaponry was not up to par with the Raiders' own ranges. The dwellers began to question the Knights' purpose for being in Urim.

"We have come due to great concerns." Orvan said. "There is a powerful darkness coming for all of us and we believe you have something that may detour it."

"We know why you've come to us." The Dweller spoke. "We know what is upon all of us."

"Then you know how important it is for us to have this artifact."

"We do. Follow me."

The Knights followed the Dweller into his much larger tent. A tent that led into a massive cave. A cave where water fell from the walls. Plant life grew boastfully. One particular plant caught the attention of Orvan.

"Wasn't aware that *juglans* grew so far out here."

"The water aids them in their growth." The Dweller said. "Plus, we enjoy them."

"I do not blame you."

It was as if they stepped into another time on the planet. The Knights were astonished. The Dweller led them toward a small spot in the cave. He removed the beast skins, unveiling a golden chest. Decorated with ancient writings and drawings. The language was much older than anything the Knights have grown to learn. Even the drawings represented creatures that haven't been seen by enashian eyes since before the Cavalier Civil War.

"Give me a hand." The Dweller said.

The Knights helped him take the chest from the opening. The chest was over six feet in length. The chest had a gold coating. Mixed with elements of *calbur*. They placed the chest down and stepped back.

"You are aware of what you're seeking?" The Dweller asked.

"We are." Novad answered.

"Good. That way you know what to do with it."

The Dweller pulled out a circular key, placing it in to eh opening on top of the chest. A small tremble echoed through the cave, originating from the chest itself. The chest clicked, with the lid pushing upward. The Dweller removed the key and opened the chest. The Knights saw something within, only covered by silk. The Dweller removed the silk, fully revealing the artifact to them. Their eyes widen as they saw it. The Dweller raised up the artifact and held it tightly. The spear point shined like new gold.

"You gaze upon a staff of Arkkon."

"Appears we do." Novad said. "Can this truly stop the darkness that is coming?"

"It will hold up well. Such parcels have proven useful throughout our history. They've ended wars and have started wars. Good and evil rests in the hands of the ones who wield them. Can we trust you in doing good with this parcel?"

"That is our sole duty." Orvan said. "It is why we are Knights of the Covenant."

The Dweller nodded and handed the staff to him. Orvan held it in awe.

"Keep it close." The Dweller said.

"How will we know when to use it?" Novad questioned.

"You will know when it tells you. That is the nature of a Parcel of Arkkon."

"Understood."

The Knights followed the Dweller to the outside and when they returned, they saw the other Knights standing. Seeing them exiting the tent with the staff. The Knights were relieved.

"They've found it." Aweran said.

"Good." Jad said. "Now we can return to Tropolton. Prepare ourselves for the Onyx Cavaliers' arrival."

The Dwellers greeted the Knights as they thanked them. The leader of the Dweller looked, measuring the Knights, but his focus was locked onto Aweran. He stared at him. Zeena looked on as the Dweller could not take his eyes off of him.

"What is it?" She asked.

"Within him, there's a disturbance. A mixture of two powerful forces. He knows not which to choose. Only the one to use when necessary."

Jad listened to the leader's words. He knew it clearly. Aweran didn't know what to make of the leader's words, only that he was telling the truth.

"How can you sense it?"

"I see the dark shadow hovering over you. You continue to ignore it as a means to causing it to flee. But it won't. only with a determined choice will it leave you alone."

Aweran took his words well. Nodding to his understanding.

"I will do my best."

"I pray you will. For your sake."

The Dweller took the moment to speak a small prayer for the Knights' safe travels. With the Knights regrouped, they rode off on their vehoes back to Coolts to reach their ship. Several minutes later, Evad Nod arrived in Urim and quickly began asking the Dwellers about the Knights. They informed him of their arrival toward Coolts to his displeasure. Evad sighed bitterly. He didn't bother being annoyed about chasing after the Knights, as it kept him off Dovan Pen's radar.

Making their way back to Coolts, they didn't waste any time returning to their ship and within minutes, they were in the air reaching the atmosphere. Once Evad had arrived, he caught a glimpse of them in orbit.

"Damn it!"

Before making a landing in Coolts, he looked outward near the docking bay and saw Dovan and his ship. Evad jolted and turned his ship around, leaving Coolts. On the bay, Dovan stood outside his ship, gazing up in the sky at Evad's ship. He glanced down toward his left forearm, the numbers moved. The clock was ticking for his capture.

CHAPTER VI

THE DEAD AMONGST THE LIVING

Sector IV, a particular region in the Stellarspace. One of galactic royalty. Such was the planet of Utomia. Home of the Navian Republic. A nation well respected by many others. The day had come when the sun rose above their lush green fields and rotating mountains. Their city glistened with light, emitting from the sun's own rays. The people of Utomia, known as the White-Haired Ones by other nations worked and took time with their families. Until the sky, which was bright became dark. The Utomians gazed up toward the sky, seeing the sun being shielded by a large dark object. The Utomians did not know what it was or could be. Only it was something of a great horror. The air turned cold to the point their breaths could be noticed. The large object above beamed a light down upon the city and within mere seconds, the city was desolated. The explosion covered many miles from the city to the mountains. Destruction was all that remained as the object vanished from their skies and the sun returned to a ruined landscape.

The Shamhuth made its travels toward Dagobar, the planet of Orchs and Trolls. The clans took immediate notice of the large ship hovering over their lands. The white light beamed down once more, destroying their valleys. But, the orchs were not like the Utomians, they gathered their forces and snatched their weapons from the armories. The clans, particularly the *Bloodaxe* and *Cavebone* clans rushed into the sunlit valley as the beam evaporated. Standing in the plains surrounded by great mountains on both sides, the two clan leaders, Thugur Suk of the Bloodaxe Clan and Thagorth of the Cavebone clan began to rally up their soldiers. Challenging those within the ship to come down and face them. From the ship appeared four battleships, lowering themselves toward the ground. The clans stepped back as the blackened ships landed. Their rusted and rotten appearances caught the orchs by shock. They weren't familiar with such technology. From their appearance, they didn't look as if they could operate. The doors of the ships slid down, facing the clans. They waited. Silence covered the grounds, until the eerie footsteps of steel hitting steel echoed. Coming from the ships were the necrofighters. Their undead appearances brought a sense of fear over the clans. Their leaders were not afraid, as they relished the chance for a battle. A total of twenty-four necrofighters were facing the orchs.

"We do not know what you are or who you are." Thugur Suk said. "But as I speak for the Bloodaxe Clan, you want a battle? We will give you a battle!"

"As will the Cavebone Clan!" Thagorth yelled. "You have no idea what you're in for!"

Thagorth slammed his battleaxe into the dirt while Thugur held his sharpened mace steady. The necrofighters wielded only their necroblades. The orch leaders screamed their battle cry and ran into battle. The necrofighers followed suit, snarling with their blades pointed forward. The battle ensued with the orchs clashing through the necrofighters with ease, for the undead warriors had no flesh. Their bones were broken easily by the orchs' strength and weaponry. It wasn't even a matter of minutes before the orchs defeated the necrofighters. Not one of them remained standing. Their skeletons displaced throughout the battleground. The orchs cheered their win. Axes, maces, and clubs held high in the air, rumbling to the roars of victory. The wind picked up, startling the orchs as it collected the skeletons. From above formed a whirlwind. The sky grew dark, just as it did on Utomia and through the whirlwind, the necrofighters returned. Their bones placed back together. Their eyes shining with a dim light.

"Come my brothers!" Thugur shouted. "Let's slaughter these toothpicks once more! This time grind their bones into dust!"

The orchs were prepared, but the necrofighters did not make a move to fight. They only stood in a single0filed lone. The orchs remained confused by their frozen state as the white light beamed down from the ship. Only this time there was an object moving through the beam, coming down in between the orchs and necrofighters. The object landed as the beam evaporated. The necrofighters instantly bowed toward the figure, leaving the orchs even more confused. The figure they were bowing to was their leader.

"You managed to defeat my soldiers without a drop of blood. Skilled warriors your kind truly are."

"Who are you?" Thugur asked.

"I am Black Hood. These are my necrofighters. We are the Onyx Cavalier Force and we've come to conquer the universe."

"You got a long way to go if you seek on conquering everything." Thagorth said. "I want to see you try and take out the Knights or those Viper Lords."

"I will have my way with them in time. Right now, you stand in my way."

Black Hood reached toward his left side, pulling out his necroblade. The glowing darkness upon the weapon startled the orchs as they've only seen such kind of weaponry in the hands of the Knights and Viper Lords. Thugur, not dismayed by the blade, slammed his axe into the ground once more, letting out a roar.

"We will not back down!"

Thagorth agreed with Thugur as their clans shouted for another battle. Black Hood grinned, looking down at his necroblade.

"As you wish."

Black Hood swung his blade, causing a large wave of necro energy to rush through the orchs, knocking them back with such a force, they flew off their feet. The barbarians were down. Some were dead as their leaders barely moved from the strong energy. Black Hood gazed own upon their bodies.

"I will not kill you both. For you are their leaders. It's better to see your warriors fall before you die. That is the way of Mors."

Thugur stood up, shaking himself from the blow. Bleeding from his chest, he still mustered the energy to raise his axe once again and Thagorth followed him. The leaders stood in front of their clans. Ready to fight for their lives. Black Hood grinned once more.

"You wish to die this day?"

"We would rather die than see such abominations rule the Stellarspace."

Black Hood sighed, wiping his necroblade with his palm.

"If that is what you desire."

Black Hood turned back toward his army, searching through them.

"Ukufa!" He yelled.

Walking through the necrofighters was one in particular. He did not appear like the others. His armor was sleek, yet not rusted. He was also cloaked with a hood. The exception being his face appeared as a skull with torn flesh. His eyes dead with a hint of life remaining. Black Hood grinned as the orch kings stepped back, seeing this lone warrior standing beside him with a similar blade to Black Hood only shorter and denser. Some would call it a Necrochete.

"This is my general Ukufa. He is like me. One of the powerful Onyx Cavaliers. Our duties are the same. Thereby, we are one."

"It's two of us and two of you." Thagorth said. "I see this as an equal opportunity"

"Unfortunately," Black Hood said, stepping aside. "This is one-on-two and this one has the advantage of victory."

Black Hood gave the command as Ukufa moved like lightning through the field, striking down the two orch kings. From there, he slaughtered the remainder of their warriors. Leaving the land to consume their blood. Above the fowls of the air began to watch as they prepared to feast. Black Hood and Ukufa returned to the ship as the necrofighters followed. Black Hood sat on his throne within the massive ship, sending out a distress call to every powerful planet in the Stellarspace.

"Living ones of the Stellarspace. I am Black Hood. Leader of the Onyx Cavalier Force. The time has come for my kind to conquer your homeworlds. Your sectors. Your lives. For the era of the Order of the

Damned has come. Utomia and Dagobar have already felt our Morsian power. Soon, your worlds will. I expect hostility from such powerful forces. Quarreling amongst yourselves will no longer suit your continued existence. I hope to see you all soon on the battlefield. Wherever it may be. For the God of the Dead has granted me this quest, and I intend on finishing it with myself on the supreme throne of the Stellarspace and our corpses corrupted as you join my armies."

CHAPTER VII

AFTERMATH OF A CATASTROPHE

With Black Hood's broadcast signaled throughout all the nations, many of them sent out a distress call to all their people. Their armies were prepared with haste. Their leaders ready to declare the location for this battle. Many of them did not take the time to think of a strategy. They just wanted a battle. To prove their rule supreme. With the nations in panic, the Council of Endro gathered themselves together and send out word toward every nation in the Stellarspace. The Council declared the Onyx Cavalier Force a dire threat to every living being and knew they must be stopped. With their word going forward for a moment of truce between conflicting planets, the Emerald Cavalier Force did not hesitate in making themselves known. The Emerald Cavaliers are the primary Cavalier Force which takes part in many battles. Seeing the Onyx Cavaliers present only gave them more hope in proving their current position.

On Moraltis, the Viper Lords began to speak with their own council. Looking for a correct answer that may benefit them in the long run. Sitting in their throne room as Supreme Cardinal Zedka entered, bowing before Obliteran and Ivah.

"I know you have such a solution to these ongoing times." Obliteran said.

"I do, my lord."

"Tell us, please." Ivah said. "What shall me and my husband do?"

"We must fight against these undead beings. Their existence only proves a threat to yours and ours. But, there is a side to this you both might not like to hear."

"Speak it anyway." Obliteran commanded.

"I would advice you both to speak with the Knights of the Covenant."

Obliteran raised up from his chair as Ivah scoffed at the words.

"I know it is not what the Dekar wilts, however, with their power, you can overcome the Onyx Cavaliers."

"Are you suggesting we align ourselves with our sworn adversaries?" Obliteran questioned. "The ones who slaughtered our predecessors?"

"Only for this short time, yes."

"Even with the Avior on their side, it would not be enough to eliminate such a powerful threat as these Onyx Cavaliers believe themselves to be."

"I understand, my lord. Which is why I would also advise you to speak with the Magus Court and the Sinstorian King concerning these matters."

Obliteran chuckled under his breath as Ivah could only shake her head in shame.

"Now, those two, I would stand by and conquer the Stellarspace. But, there is a cost in that. The Magus Court only seeks what they desire. Their magic ruling all. The Sinistorian King is too conflicted with his own matters."

"You speak of the governmental shifts in Sinstor? I am aware."

"Anyhow, we will speak to them both." Obliteran said. "We'll head out to Ordow for an audience with the Master Wizard. Afterwards, we'll ravel to Sinstor and see what their king wishes for his people."

Zedka bowed, leaving the throne room. Obliteran sighed as Ivah stood up from her seat, approaching the large window behind the seats. Gazing out toward the grey sky.

"Are you sure this is a good plan?" Ivah asked.

"It is the best we have at the moment."

"And Those of the Avior? Shall we speak to them as well?"

Obliteran sighed. Tapping his fingers on the armrest.

"We'll talk to them last. That way, if they decline, we'll already have an army on our side."

Back on Helio, the Knights gathered themselves together, for they were already set on facing the Onyx Cavaliers. Aweran, waited for the day as he could not sleep for the dream continued to haunt him. Yet, he never appeared physically tired as the Avior had sustained him. The Knights had grouped together in Temple of the Avior where Ocha waited for them. Jad had presented the Staff of Arkkon to Ocha to examine it. The Elder Knight touched the staff and felt its power. A power surging on its own as if was the origin of its own creation.

"This Parcel has power." Ocha proclaimed. "A power that should be handled carefully."

"How do we use it against the Onyx Cavaliers?" Aweran questioned.

"As you do all other weapons. Do not forget, this Staff is a weapon of war. Only to be wielded in the right hands."

"So what you're saying is, we take the Staff and impale their leader with it?" Zeena asked.

"Precisely." Ocha answered. "Did you expect something more cryptic? With this Parcel, it is as easy as going into combat with your blades."

"The only question now is who will wield it into batle." Amzi said. "Elder Ocha, do you have anyone in mind?"

Ocha looked out among the Knights and nodded with a smile.

"The one who shall wield this into battle is none other than Aweran himself. For he gave us the news of their coming. Seeing it before time. Henceforth, he must be the one to take it into battle and slay this Black Hood. Killing him will slaughter the entire Onyx Cavalier Force by default."

Aweran nodded with a growing sense of breath. The pressure for saving the entire Stellarspace had slowly started to grow on his shoulders.

"I must add, you all will not be enough. You'll need to go out and

35

speak with the other nations. Those we have trust with. See if they're willing to join you in this battle. For they should, even their worlds are in danger of being destroyed."

"We'll head out to speak with the Ard-King on Endor." Jad said. "I'm sure he will be willing lend us some of his Ard-Knights into this battle."

"What about the Elladians?" Zeena asked. "I'm sure they would be willing to help us."

"You have a point, Knightess." Ocha said. "You have your duties. Now go. There is no time to waste."

The Knights took their leave from the temple. Jad turned around toward Ocha.

"This is not just a battle we're heading for, my Elder. It is a war. A war for all life."

"Yes it is."

"If I may ask, it would benefit us all if you were to join us."

Ocha began to laugh. Hearing Jad's words carefully. Ocha, even in his ancient age could find humor in the most dreadful of times. He quieted himself steadily.

"Do not fret yourself, Elder Jad Serkelod. All good things come in time."

Jad heard the words and bowed his head.

"I will take your word for it."

The Knights went and prepared their Helio Sor ships. While working on one, Aweran and Zeena began to discuss the circumstance of confronting Black Hood and Aweran's lack of rest. Aweran warned Zeena she had nothing to concern herself with, for the Avior was taking care of him and she knew it to be true. But even she could not deny the tiny seed of doubt that lingered in Aweran's mind. An opening for the Dekar to slip in if it had the chance. Finishing up in the ship, a signal came forth from the comms. Aweran and Zeena took a listen, hearing a faint voice coming through the static.

"Is…anyone here.. Calling… for… ssistance."

"You recognize that voice?" Zeena asked.

"I do. It's Evad."

Aweran worked on the signaling system until the voice came through clearly.

"Evad, do you hear me?" Aweran said. "Evad, can you hear me?"

"I hear you." Evad responded. "Wait, is that Aweran?"

"It is. Good to hear your voice again, old friend."

"Ah! Ha! Same here. Same here."

"Why are you contacting us?" Zeena asked.

"Zeena's there too? Ah, things must be going well for the both of you."

"They are." Aweran said. "But, tell us what's going on? You sound like you're in trouble?"

"I am in a sort of trouble. I need some help."

"Is it the Onyx Cavaliers?"

"Those undead freaks? No. something more lively. Being hunted down by one of the Pen Family's Venators. He's coming closer to catching me."

"What do you need us to do?"

"Get the damn jackal off my back. Anyway you can."

Aweran turned to Zeena as the two began to think. They know Evad 's skills are useful and they're in a current situation where they'll need every hand they can gather to face the Onyx Cavaliers. They both nodded, thinking of the same idea.

"We'll help you if you can aid us in return."

"I'm all in. what do you guys need help with?"

"Facing the Onyx Cavaliers. Are you up for it?"

"Well, that will clear up my schedule from fleeing the Pen Venator. Where are you guys? Still on Helio?"

"Yes. Where are you?"

"Hiding on Erets-Alpha at the moment. In the city of Aelhaven. It isn't hard to find."

"Keep yourself ready. Zeena and I will be coming to get you."

"I'll be waiting, old friend."

The comms went off as Aweran walked outside of the ship toward Elder Amzi and Elder Jad. He began explaining to them the call and how valuable Evad could be to the ongoing cause. The Knights approved of more fighters, giving Aweran and Zeena permission to head out to Erets-

Alpha.

"Aweran." Jad said. "Make sure this Venator doesn't track your ship. We don't need anymore trouble to deal with. Especially with a Venator of such stature."

"Understood, grandfather."

The Helio Sor ship lifted from the ground and took off into the atmosphere.

Elsewhere in the Stellarspace, the Viper Lords had arrived on the planet of Ordow to meet with the Magus Court with their Sinth-Tred. The colors of blue, red, and violet surround the atmosphere of the planet. The Viper Lords knew of the knowledge to avoid the beautiful sight of the planet, for it is known to deceive foreigners as they enter the planet's atmosphere. As the Sinth-Tred dove through the colorful skies, entering the cold and dark landscape of the planet. They looked ahead, seeing the tall, dark tower in the distance.

"There." Obliteran pointed. "That is where we must land."

The aeronauts piloted the ship toward the tower as violet lighting struck through the sky. They reached the ship, landing on the opening pad. The Viper Lords exited the ship just as six sorcerers stepped out of the tower. The strange scent of cinnamon mixed with electricity filled the air as the presence of magic could be strongly felt as they breathed in the air. Obliteran and Ivah approached the sorcerers as Zedka stepped forward, declaring the Viper Lords' arrival to Ordow.

"The Lords of the Viper have come here to seek an audience with the Magus Court. This is of an urgent matter."

The sorcerers remained silent, facing one another in a quiet conversation. Zedka turned toward the Viper Lords with only confusion. Obliteran sighed, raising up his Sinthblade.

"Let us pass. This is not the time to delay."

The sorcerers saw the blade and raised their right hands. Permitting them to enter the tower. Obliteran was pleased, sheathing the blade as they walked toward the gates of the tower. Magic was drenched upon them as it was on the ground. Every step they took, particles of electric magic sparked under their feet. They entered the tower and the sorcerers paused in their steps, blocking their entry.

"What is the issue?" Zedka asked.

"They must leave their weapons here." One sorcerer spoke.

"I do not understand."

"It is the custom of the Magus Court. All foreigners must obey these laws if they intend on leaving with their lives."

"Are you threatening us?" Ivah questioned. "Do you know who we are and what we can do?"

"Yes. We do." said a voice coming from within the tower.

Walking past the sorcerers, was one of the Magus Court. A supreme member of the court due to his violet and scarlet apparel. His hood was decorated with jewels of the ground. He held his hands up.

"There's no need for violence. Not yet anyway."

"We do not have time to waste." Obliteran said. "We must speak to the Master Wizard. It is urgent."

"I know. We know. Please follow me. And keep your weapons."

The Viper Lords nodded as they followed the Supreme Wizard into the council room. They stood in the center as around them appeared the Magus Court. All three members. Approaching from the center was the Master Wizard himself. His head held high as his eyes laid upon the Viper Lords.

"Ah. I see Those of the Dekar have come to our dwelling place. What is the cause this day?"

"Master Wizard of the Magus Court, I am Supreme Cardinal Zedka and I speak for the Viper Lords. We are here because of a terrible threat that is currently roaming the Stellarspace."

"What is this threat you speak of?" One of the Wizards asked.

"The Onyx Cavalier Force is here. They've already attacked two planets and are seeking the rest. Including ours and yours."

The Master Wizard scoffed without feeling.

"You're telling us that a Cavalier Force is seeking to destroy every planet in the Stellarspace?"

"Yes. But these are not like the others. The Onyx Cavaliers are…dead."

"Dead? How can they be dead when you're here speaking of them in great concern?" The second Wizard asked.

"These Cavaliers are undead." Obliteran said. "They have already felt the spark of life exit their bodies. They originate from the planet Mors. A dead planet in of itself."

The Master Wizard rose in his seat, staring at Obliteran and Ivah. He measured them both with his eyes as his pupils shifted in colors.

"What happened to Sinth Cain and Sinth Kara?"

"Their lives were ended on Ro. By the Knights of the Covenant."

"Ah. Why not seek revenge for your fallen predecessors. Leave this undead force to the other nations to deal with."

"Because the Knights will be involved in this affair." Zedka said. "It will take all of us to eliminate the Onyx Cavaliers. We can return to our normal events afterwards."

"I see. What you ask of is our help in this matter?"

"If we don't do anything, the Onyx Cavaliers will be coming here soon."

"I know." The Master Wizard said. "Let us speak on the matter briefly. We'll give you an answer once it's upon us."

The Wizard raised his hand, forming a magical field over the Viper Lords. Covering them from hearing anything outside of it. Obliteran went to reach for his aduroblade, only to be stopped by Zedka.

"Give it a moment."

The Lords waited as they watched the Magus Court talk. Within a minute, the force field fell apart into embers as the wizards sat in their seats.

"Very well, by our laws and for the protection of our planet, we will assist you in defeating this undead force. Only to ensure our place in the Stellarspace."

"We do it for the same cause." Zedka said. "We will take our leave now."

"I have something else to ask." Obliteran said. "How will you aid us in this battle? Will you join in on the fight yourselves or will some of your sorcerers come fight for the cause?"

"You have no reason to worry. The Warlocks of the West wind will assist you in this battle. For if Ordow is indeed threatened, they will make sure to threat is exterminated."

Obliteran looked around the council room. Even gazing up toward the star-lit ceiling.

"Where are these Warlocks?"

"They are here. They are everywhere on Ordow. You will see them when the time comes. Now, leave our planet. We'll do well on our side of the deal. Make sure you do the same with your own."

Obliteran grinned with a slight scoff.

"Don't worry yourself, Wizard. The Dekar will see us through."

"The Dekar?" The Master Wizard said. "Only sorcery is the true power in the universe."

"We'll see soon."

The Viper Lords left the tower and did not waste anymore time on Ordow as they left the planet.

Their next stop was Sinstor, to meet with the Sinstorian King. Entering the atmosphere and coming through the clouds as below them laid lush fields and dunes as far as one could see. Arriving in the city of Misriaym, the capital city of the planet. Flying over the Yeor Waterlands as the Yeor Dragons swam across, the Sinth-Tred landed near the palace where Pharao Hophra-Apr waited. Receiving their notice some time earlier, the Viper Lords and the Pharao talked inside of the golden palace concerning the Onyx Cavaliers. The Sinstorians knowing of their shared history with the Viper Lords, Pharao Kophra agreed to help in the upcoming battle.

"It is a pity how your predecessors fell at the hands of the Covenant Ones. Yet, the war between their Avior and your Dekar goes as far back as before the birth of Sinstorian rule."

"I will send out my best warriors to assist you in this battle." Pharao Kophra said. "Give us the call when the location is known. My warriors will be on their way."

"Will you not join us?" Ivah questioned. "It will instill great strength in your warriors if you are on the battlefield with us."

"I would. However, the ongoing conflict between Sinstor and Sidhu greatly needs my gaze."

"You're at war with the Sidhuians?" Zedka asked. "When did this begin?"

"Some mere months ago. Concerns over rules and location. We have our way. Hey have theirs. A disagreement came when several of my warriors were found dead. We returned the favor and thus, the war between our two planets began."

"You could've contacted our predecessors." Obliteran said. "They would've helped you in the matter."

"I'll rather handle this on my own. Sidhu is small, yet has potential to be even stronger. I cannot allow them to prosper over us."

"I get the sentiment."

"I understand." Ivah nodded.

"We will be waiting for your warriors when the time comes, Pharao." Obliteran said. "We will give the call."

"I know you will. Sinstorians and Moraltians have never let each other down. I do not intend for us to start this day."

"May your gods guide your rule." Obliteran nodded.

"And may your god give you strength."

The Viper Lords left the planet of Sinstor, heading off to their next location.

Aweran and Zeena had returned to Erets-Alpha, making their travel to the city of Aelhaven. Aelhaven is no Coolts. For it is a city derived from conflicts and underground dealers. Aelhaven is similar to Erac, aside from the crowded presence of Star Raiders. Aelhaven is the place for particular Venators, Rangers, Strikefighters, Mercenaries, and Assassins. Bounties are made in this city. Payments are always a daily occurrence. It was nightfall when the two Knights had arrived, receiving a signal that Evad was inside one of the clubs. Bothered by such an environment, they found the location centered in the middle of the city. The club was surrounded by mercenaries, looking for new jobs to take. Whether it was to eliminate high-profile targets or even stealing ships belonging to the Viper Order.

"He's here." Aweran said.

"Let's go and find him."

They approached the club doors, only to be stopped by a *mechroid* bouncer. Bulky and lean in appearance. Made of metal and coated in calbur. Aweran appeared displeased, seeing as how the residents of the city use mechroids to do such occupations. The mechroid stretched its right arm, blocking their entrance into the club. From its hands formed a baton. Aweran reached for his aduroblade, only to be blocked by Zeena. Her eyes turned to him and he saw her look. With a low sigh, he removed his hand from the hilt and stepped back.

"We're here looking for a friend." Zeena said. "He told us he was in this club."

"That correct?" The mechroid said.

"It is. Once we find me, we'll be out of here. No problems."

The mechroid nodded in agreement and stood aside, permitting them entrance. As they walked in, Zeena suggested Aweran relax, however he could not as time was a factor to him greatly. The less time remaining, the closer his dream becomes a reality. Within the club were a great many mercenaries. Venators hanging around on the left side of the club. Rangers and Strikefighters socializing on the right side of the club. Aweran gazed out toward the right side, spotting a man wearing a hat and trench coat. sitting at a table by himself. He recognized him from the badge he wore on his left arm. The sigil of a range.

"There he is." Aweran said, pointing.

"Let's go meet him."

They walked past the crowds of Rangers and Strikefighters. Some of the Venatores knew them to be Knights, sensing their aura and noticing their choice of apparel. They reached the table as Aweran slammed his palm atop it. The man jolted, raising up the brim of his hat to see them. It was Evad.

"Holy High!" Evad said, jumping from his seat to hug them. "Damn fine good to see you both! And in the flesh no doubt!"

"I could say the same about you." Zeena said.

"Same here." Aweran said. "You contacted us."

Evad looked around the club for anything unusual that he may notice. Finding nothing, he asked them to sit and they sat.

"I did and I am thankful for you both coming. I tried to reach you guys when you were here earlier."

"What do you mean?" Aweran asked.

"I've been on y'all's trail since you last left. I heard you guys were in Erac. Went there and they told me you went south. Down around Urim. Came there, they said you were heading to Coolts to leave the planet. Went to Coolts, you guys were already gone."

"Why were you looking for us?" Zeena said. "You mentioned something about being hunted?"

"There's this Venator on my trail. A descendant of the Pen family. He's been onto me for the past three years. He's heard about my actions on Thran. The Battle of Thran that is. Wants to pick up the pieces from the Dos Ar-Suyaza that we dealt with."

"That was sixty years ago." Aweran said. "Why use something from then to do business?"

Aweran nodded, looking at Zeena as the conversations of the club covered their own.

"We can help you, Evad.' Aweran said. "As long as you aid us in a matter."

"You had mentioned the Onyx Cavalier Force." Evad said, shaking his head. "I saw the broadcast. Those guys really dead?"

"Yes." Zeena said. And if they have their way, we'll all be."

Evad nodded, taking a drink of *shehar* from his mug. Sighing as he lowered the mug. He placed his hat perfectly atop his head and stood up from the table.

"Then let's go."

They stood up, following him to the exit. Walking outside, Evad said his ship was at the hangar near the exit of Aelhaven. They told him to meet them in the atmosphere. Evad agreed and the ships took off into the night sky. With the ships in the heavens, Dovan Pen stepped out of the club, staring into the night sky. Through his helmet, he could see through the dark sky and saw Evad's ship.

The Helio Sor and Evad's ship, the *Strike Rider* hovered in the atmosphere. Evad wondered why he had to meet them there as opposed to traveling to another plant. Aweran stated they must travel to Endor in haste as the other Knights are waiting for them. Evad sighed.

"Endor. That place is cold, you know."

"We'll need their aid in fighting the Onyx Cavalier. Besides, The Pen Venator won't be able to come for you there. Endorian rules work differently than anywhere else."

Evad nodded with a smirk.

"Good to know."

"Let's get going." Zeena said.

Both ships took off in hyper speed, instantly taking them to the atmosphere of Endor.

CHAPTER VIII

THE ARD-KING AND THE ELLADIAN QUEEN

The cold air of Endor blew across the ships as they could feel the air.

"Told you guys it was too damn cold." Evad said, over the comms.

Looking in the distance below, they saw the Helio Sor ships of the Knights parked in front of the Gate of Regnum. Evad looked and saw the castle that awaited them.

"That place is massive." Evad said. "How come other nations don't try and take this place as among the others?"

"Because this planet is covered with energy beyond their own technology." Zeena said. "You've heard the tales of how the *Carusian Ore* is one of the most sought after mineral in all the Stellarspace."

"I have. Stuff's too hard to come by."

"Maybe you can ask them once we're down there." Aweran said.

"Perhaps I will."

They lowered and landed their ships. Stepping out of them to face the tall gate. In front of the gate stood two Watchmen. Aweran, Zeena, and Evad approached them. The Watchmen looked at them, seeing their Knights apparel before turning to Evad. He stretched his arms.

"What's the problem?"

"Two Knights of the Covenant and a Ranger?"

"We're here on important matters." Aweran said. "I'm sure the other Knights mentioned our arrival."

"No worries. They did. Enter."

The Gate opened as they entered. The Watchmen kept their eyes heavily on Evad as the Gate closed. Now, they were approaching the castle of the Ard-Kings, the *Regnum Caelorum*. Outside of the castle, they saw the Ard-Knights in their light-blue metal armor training as well as the Gentlemen of Ard, dressed in their robes going about their business. Evad was astounded by the amount of people he saw. Questioning how they manage to live in a place with such coldness. Before they entered, they stood and saw the three statues of the three gods of Endor. The *Regnum Trinitas*. *All-Father Ard*, *Son-Ard*, and *Spirit of Ard*. The statues were constructed in a mix of stone and ice. Evad was impressed as Aweran and Zeena shook themselves. For such imagery is considered idolatry to the Knights of the Covenant.

Walking past the statues, they entered the castle, seeing Elder Jad standing by speaking with one of the Ardguards. Jad looked to see them and greeted them.

"You made it." Jad said. "Good. Who's this guy?"

"This is Evad Nod. He helped us sixty years ago during the Battle of Thran. He's a good friend."

"I see. Well, I don't usually trust Rangers. But, if you're a help to our cause, so be it."

"I understand your reasons." Evad said. "I'm not one to cause trouble. In a bad way that is."

"Have you spoken to their king about aiding us?" Aweran asked.

"I was just about to do that."

The Ardguard approached Jad and the others.

"His Majesty, The Ard-King will see you now."

Jad nodded.

"Let's go speak to the king."

Aweran, Zeena, and Evad followed Jad and Amzi into the throne room where they saw the Ard-King waiting. Standing beside the king was one of his clergymen. The clergyman was known in Endor as one of the Deacons of Ard. He stepped forward between the Ard-King and the Knights.

"On this day, you speak with the wonderful, the glorious, the powerful Ansfried-Ard! Ard-King of Endor!"

Ansfried-Ard waved his hand as Evad could only marvel at the sight of the king's crown of ice. The Deacon bowed before the Ard-King before taking his leave. Ansfried stood up from his throne and approached Jad and Amzi, hugging them like brothers.

"It has been sometime." Ansfried said.

"It has." Jad replied. "I'm sorry we didn't have time to warn you earlier about our sudden arrival."

"You're here now. All is well."

Aweran, Zeena, and Evad stepped forward to greet the king. Ansfried greeted Aweran and Zeena with kindness. His eyes touched Evad and his smile began to fade.

"Who let a Ranger into my castle?"

"He's here with us." Aweran said. "Apologies, Ard-King, but he proves a useful help to what's happening."

Ansfried stared at Evad. Taking a moment before sighing.

"Very well. Just make sure he doesn't take anything. I know these Ranger types. No different than Venators."

Evad lifted up his finger.

"Well, some of us are more honorable than others."

"Save your words. Before your life is taken by one of my Ard-Knights."

Ansfried returned to his chair.

"Now, why is it that you've all come to Endor?"

"Because of the dire threat that awaits us all out in the Stellarspace." Amzi said. "You saw the broadcast."

"I did. I do not fear those undead fools. Let them come to Endor. They'll suffer the same fate as Blath the Wicked."

"We have a plan." Jad said.

"What is this plan of yours?"

"To gather as much aid as we can. Then, once we have enough, we will send out a response to them. Stating where they can meet us to end this. A perfect way to save more lives."

"Where is this place you are preparing to meet them?"

"Our choice was the planet Zappdow." Jad said. "No enashians or any life forms that we know of live there as the environment is too hostile. It's a perfect place for such a battle."

"A planet that is constantly drenched in thunderstorms with

tremendous heat? Might work. However, I thought Thran would be the obvious choice. It is the Planet of Wars after all."

"Yes. But the Onyx Cavaliers would know that already if they wanted us there." Amzi noted.

"Fair point of observation. Now, how am I supposed to help in this matter?"

"Lend us some of your Ard-Knights." Jad said. "Only a hundred of them."

Ansfried took a moment to think. Standing up from his chair and pacing slowly in the throne room. The Knights stood and waited for his response. Ansfried paused in his steps and let out a slow sigh before sitting.

"Very well. As a favor to our everlasting brotherhood, I will lend you a hundred of my Ard-Knights. I do not concern myself with their safekeeping. Their training under the best of instructors. They know how to deal in battle when it comes to any enemy."

"But, these enemies are dead." Evad said. "Undead I might add."

Ansfried did not reply to Evad.

Thank you, Ard-King." Jad said.

"Call me Ansfried, Jad. You know this already."

"I do. Only out of respect." Jad nodded.

"How soon will you need my knights?"

"Once we have everything in place, we'll send out word." Amzi said.

"I take it your son won't be joining us?" Jad questioned.

"Eudo is ready for war. Yet, he's no Siegfried-Ard. He isn't prepared for. Perhaps the next battle that comes to our doorsteps."

"Understandable." Jad nodded.

"I myself would join you in this fight. But, my time is drawing thin. Soon, I'll be with my forefathers in the Sleeping Room of Kings.

"Wasn't going to say it, but, you are looking a little old." Jad smiled.

"Look who's talking."

"Fair. Fair." Jad shook his head. "We have one more stop to make before we return to Helio."

"Where are we headed next?" Aweran asked.

"To speak with Queen Herena on Ellada. See if she'll let her Marvels

49

accompany us into battle."

"The Herenian Empire will sure be happy to get involved." Ansfried said. "War is their nature."

"You're right on that." Amzi said. "Good to see you again, Ansfried."

"I bid you Knights and your Ranger well on your travels." Ansfried said. "See that these Onyx Cavaliers receive what they deserve."

"That we will." Jad said as they exited the throne room.

The Knights left the castle, returning to their ships at the Gate. From there, they flew back into the atmosphere and hyper sped into the skies of Ellada.

Seeing the golden colors of the skies of Ellada, the ships made their landing in Olympya. Staring at the Palace of Herena up ahead as they saw the Marvels of the Universe training with Queen Herena's daughter, Princess Savan-Nah. While walking toward the palace, Evad took notice of no men in sight.

"You wondering why?" Amzi asked.

"Yeah. I've heard the stories. I just didn't believe them."

"There are men on this planet. Just on a different continent."

"Do tell."

"Ever heard of the *Ostacrean War?*"

"I have not."

"You'll have to learn up on it. Explains everything."

Walking up the stairs to the Palace doors. The guards stood forward, holding their staves against the visitors. Amzi and Jad pressed forward, showing they come with urgency and not conflict. The guards take notice and proceed to allow them entry. Inside the palace, they could see the golden decorations of statues dedicated to Queen Herena and the Marvels. Large scrolls on the walls depicting their battles across history. Some against other nations and some against their own people. One of the guards led them into the throne room where Queen Herena remained. Sitting on the tall throne, she looked down at the Knights and smiled.

"How fitting for the Knights of the Covenant to grant their presence to me."

"Queen Herena," Jad said. "We come here urgently. As you may know, the threat from the Onyx Cavalier Force. They seek to decimate all living beings and rule the Stellarspace as their own."

"And you've come to ask of my aid in this battle? Against the undead force?"

"We do."

Queen Herena stood up and walked down the steps toward them. She stood before them in her garments of royalty. So much gold if a light would shine upon her, it could very well blind anyone.

"You really came here to ask if I would allow my Marvels into another war. A war that derives on the fate of all living beings including Elladians?"

"Yes." Amzi said. "We would not be here otherwise."

"You'll have my Marvels."

"Wait." Jad said. "You're serious?"

"I am. Unlike you Covenant Knights, us Elladians thrive on warfare. It is in our blood. My Marvels will meet you at the location and my daughter will be accompanying them."

"Thank you, Queen Herena." Amzi said.

"Now go. Before I change my mind and have them wage war on you instead."

The Knights listened and took their leave from the palace. Ansfried was correct in his words regarding Queen Herena. With enough warriors on their side, the Knights returned to Helio in preparation for the following day, as the battle against the Onyx Cavaliers was nigh.

During the night, Aweran remained awake as he could not sleep due to the recurring nightmare. He took one look at the Staff of Arkkon. Preparing his mind of what's to come. He went into his prayer room and fell on his knees.

"*O' High One.* Your power and your strength are needed in these times. On the morrow, we head out to war with the Onyx Cavalier Force. With enough fighters on our side, I believe we can win this battle. I only ask that you guide us through the coming war and see that the Knights remain and all life is victorious. As in all things, Your will be done."

CHAPTER IX

THE BATTLE OF ZAPPDOW

The next morning on Helio, the Knights were prepared. Heading for their Helio Sor ships as they gathered themselves for the battle ahead. Not all of the Knights were going to war, as Helio needed many of them to stay behind to protect the planet from any other threats that may present themselves. Everyone who were set to travel for Zappdow were Aweran, Zeena, Jad, Amzi, Ebed, Novad, Orvan, and Evad. Their ships were ready as they rose to the sky and took off into the atmosphere.

Through the hyper speed, the Knights arrived at Zappdow. The planet covered in dark clouds as streaks of lightning gave it brightness. The ships flew through the clouds, moving quickly past the bolts. Making their landing on a mountain range, overlooking a large valley. When the Knights exited their ships, they were instantly hit with a gust of wind blowing exceedingly high temperatures. Evad took off his hat to wipe the sweat from his forehead.

"Now I know why no one comes to this place. Are you sure this was the right spot to have this battle?"

"It was a different choice to make." Aweran said. "I guess you wanted to return to Thran once more. Like last time."

"Thran might've had volcanoes and the like, but it didn't have heat like this. Nor did it have thunderstorms over our heads."

Jad stepped forward, seeing the valley. He pointed toward it as they made their way into it. Once they were standing in the valley, they saw how massive it was. How wide it was. Nearly every army from every nation could fit in that valley and not have a worry about space.

"I take it this place has a name?" Evad asked.

"The *Valley of Hazum*." Amzi said.

Jad pulled out one of contactors, giving everyone a look. They knew what he was about to do and without fail, Jad pressed the button on the contactor, calling for all their allies to join them in Zappdow. The signal went out and they waited. Several minutes later, the sky beamed open as the Ard-Legion, one of the superior groups of Ard-Knights made their arrival in their Regnum-Streakers. On the other side of the sky came Princess Savan-Nah and the Marvels of the Universe, riding down on their Star Horses. Coming behind them, surprising the Knights were the starships of the Novar Force of Utomia.

"Guess they want payback." Evad nodded.

Landing their ships on the other mountain ranges throughout the region, they made their arrival into he valley. Greeting the Knights and Evad.

"Queen Herena told us of your petition." Princess Savan-Nah said. "We're here to see it through."

"Thank you, Princess." Jad said. "You and your Marvels will be greatly needed."

Coming down the hill with the Novar Force was its namesake. Dressed in his sapphire-made armor as his long white hair flew through the heated winds. He approached the Knights and nodded.

"Didn't think you would show up." Amzi said.

"Those undead ones attacked my world first. I will see them have such recompense for their actions."

"Speaking of them, where are they?" Novad asked.

"They'll arrive once everyone is here." Jad said. "We're just waiting on some others."

"Like who?" Zeena questioned. "Everyone we've contacted have arrived."

"No." Amzi said. "Not everyone."

The air around them became tense, even Aweran readied himself, sensing something related to an enemy. They all felt it and once they gazed up toward the thundering sky, the clouds moved aside for the arrival of the Viper Lords, the Magus Court, the Sinstorian Army, and the glowing, shiny Light and brooding, glaring Dark Elves of Sudravor. The Sinth-Tred ship landed, and they waited as Sinth Obliteran and Sinth Ivah arrived on the valley grounds.

"Surprised to see you two." Aweran said.

"Don't suit yourself clean." Obliteran said. "We have a common enemy. Once this is done, we'll be back to finish you off."

Arriving with the Magus Court also was Gaulhan the Wizard. He saw Aweran and Zeena and greeted them with kindness.

"It's been a long time."

"It has." Zeena said. "Did the Magus Court put you up to this?"

"I heard of this undead force and their threat rule all life. I could not sit by and allow them to continue. This day, their plans come to an end."

Gaulhan took notice of Aweran holding the Staff of Arkkon. Sensing the energy pouring from it as it even affected his own magic staff.

"Where did you get that?"

"From a secret place." Aweran answered. "It will be of use in this battle."

Gaulhan knew its purpose and only nodded with a smile. While everyone was getting acquainted, Novar approached Amzi and Jad while looking up to the clouds.

"Where are they? He asked. "Where are those undead destroyers?"

"I am about to call them out." Jad said. "It will bring them here. Once then, the battle shall begin."

"I'm ready." Novar said, pulling out his Utomian Blade.

Jad gathered everyone around as he told them of his next action. Hearing his words, they were ready. The Rainshockers loaded. The Magus Court beaming with sorcery. The Sinstorian Army sharpening their swords and spears. The Elves cleaning their rapiers. The Novar Force building up their galactic energy. Princess Savan-Nah and the Marvles began chanting a war cry. The Ard-Legion stomping the grounds with their feet. The Viper Lords raising up their aduroblades as the Knights did the same. Evad shrugged, holding up his range.

Jad began broadcasting the signal of their location into the

Stellarspace.

The signal went forward and without fail, the Onyx Cavaliers caught it, seeing the beacon set on Zappdow while hearing Jad's voice calling them forward for battle. A war for the Stellarspace as it was declared. Black Hood, sitting on his throne smirked.

"We make for Zappdow. Preparing the portal."

The sky of Zappdow grew darker. Not of the clouds above. Even the lightning began to grow dim and only darkness remained. Everyone on the valley grounds waited as the clouds were quickly shoved back as if pushed by a large gust of wind. The Shamhuth had arrived. Along with it was the *Perisher*, Black Hood's own starship.

"I'll be damned." Evad said, looking up to the ships.

The Shamhuth opened beneath and out of it came the moving ships of the necrofighters. Beaming down toward the valley with attacks. Everyone rounded up as the battle had begun. The Knights moved with haste while the Magus Court summoned their sorcery to deflect the striking blasts from the necrofighters' ships.

"Aweran, Zeena." Jad said. "This is it. Ready yourselves!"

They nodded before turning to each other.

"Whatever happens, remember I love you." Zeena said.

"Don't speak like that. This Staff will make sure you won't die this day. Nor will I."

The necrofighters landed and came out of their ships like ravaging animals. Attacking anyone in their sight. Obliteran and Ivah were not afraid, using their aduroblades to slash through the coming necrofighters with ease.

"The Fallen One will be pleased." Ivah said, grinning.

"Yes, He will."

Rainshockers began firing their plasma-ranges at the necrofighters. Evad followed them with his own as he ran through the valley. The Knights clashed against the necrofighters as there were over dozens of them in the valley. Lightning began to strike on the ground, giving them some assistance as the necrofighters were not aware of the storms. The Perisher made its landing near the valley on a cliff and out of it arrived both Black Hood and Ukufa. Aweran looked up toward the cliff, seeing Black Hood.

"It's him." Aweran pointed.

Zeena and Jad looked ahead, seeing him hovering toward the valley grounds with his necroblade out and ready for the fight. Ukufa ran through the air life stairs with his necrochete ready. He leaped into the air and with a graveling roar, he plunged the chete into the ground, causing a tremor knocking everyone nearby back. Novar protected himself with a force field as did Gaulhan.

"You first." Novar told Gaulhan.

"I thought royalty always made the first moves."

"On this occasion, I offer the first shot to you."

Gaulhan moved through the crowded valley with ease, crashing his staff against Ukufa's necrochete. On the other side, Novar arrived with his blade, going for a strike against Ukufa's back. The undead warrior saw him coming and quickly caught the blade in his left hand. Roaring toward the Utomian Prince. While Evan shot down many necrofighters, the sound of a jetpack caught his ear. Something landed behind him and as he turned, seeing the armored figure and his plasma-range aimed. He sighed bitterly.

"Come on."

"You thought I wasn't going to find you." Dovan Pen said.

"Look around you. There are much more important things happening here!"

"I see that." Dovan said, shooting down an incoming necrofighter. "But, I've come for you. The bounty is just too good."

Evad and Dovan began firing at each other through the crowds. Both firing several shots at the necrofighters without ever giving them an eye as they were interfering in their conflict as they took more shots at one another.

In the sky, more necrofighters arrived in their starships, giving way for the eglahs to arrive and take the conflict to the skies. The Ard-Legion followed them.

Gaulhan and Novar had a more difficult time holding Ukufa back as his power grew. Black Hood reached the ground and quickly took down several of the Elves, rain shockers, and Ard-Knights. The Marvels charged toward him with their swords and he only waved his hands, causing a massive rift of wind to knock them back. Black Hood was only focused on Aweran and Zeena. They saw him hovering toward them as Aweran told Zeena to stay behind him. She quickly refused as she held up her adurostaff. Aweran followed, raising up his aduroblade in preparation.

"It is astounding to finally see you both. Eye-to-eye."

"You will not kill my wife." Aweran said. "You will not."

"The future is clear, young Serkelrod. It is I who shall bring it forward. Thus, changing the landscape of all the nations to see. The Stellarspace shall be mine as it will belong to the God of the Dead."

"There is only one true god, Black Hood and he will grant us the victory."

Black Hood grinned as he and Aweran clashed blades. The thunder quickened the air as the bolting sound rushed from them. Zeena rushed forward, seeking to impale Black Hood, but his gaze was too quickly seeing her adurostaff incoming, he shoved Aweran back and grabbed the staff, throwing her across the valley grounds.

"Zeena!"

"Don't worry yourself. She is not dead. Yet."

Jad ran forward, striking Black Hood with his aduroblade. Zeena arose from the ground, looking toward them as three necrofighters were running to her. She stood up, twirling the adurostaff and slashing her way through them as their torsos flew through the air. Ukufa arrived to attack Jad, only for Aweran to push him back and attack with his aduroblade. Striking Ukufa's necrochete. Black Hood looked around, finding himself cornered by Zeena, Sinth Ivah, Princess Savan-Nah, and Gaulhan. He grinned.

"So I see. A Knightess of the Covenant, a Viper Lord, an Elladian princess, and a wizard seek to ruin my plans. How pathetic."

"You are of the unnatural order, fiend." Gaulhan said as his staff began to charge with magic. "This day, you shall be put down into the dirt where you belong."

"Very well then. I'm waiting."

While the four of them dealt with Black Hood. Evad and Dovan continued their shootout. Killing many necrofighters in their way as they continued to take shots. Dovan was becoming impatient as he missed several rounds at Evad.

"You're only delaying the inevitable."

"I think that would be best."

Evad moved, using the necrofighters as shields from Dovan's plasma rounds. Evad rushed toward him, dropkicking him to the ground before kicking his range to the side.

"You dare!"

"Yeah I do."

Evad fired a shot into Dovan's chest armor, powering down the energy source to his jetpack.

"Good luck dealing with these undead folks!"

"I am not done with you."

"I know. Unless you can handle these necrofighters, I'll give you another shot at another time.

"This is not over."

"I know. I know."

Before Dovan could raise up to attack Evad, a small army of necrofighters charged at him. Blocking him from reaching Evad. Dovan shouted in anger as a calbur blade appeared from his right forearm, slicing away at the undead army. Evad watched on and ran off from the site, returning to the larger battle.

Meanwhile, Ukufa found himself in a similar situation. Staring at

Aweran, Obliteran, Novar, and the Master Wizard. Ukufa grunted toward them like an animal trapped. Obliteran chuckled as he raised his aduroblade.

"I can take this one." Obliteran said, aiming his aduroblade.

"Don't be so egotistical, Moraltian." Novar said. "I will have this fight."

"Enough of this bickering." Master Wizard said. "I will handle this abomination."

Ukufa lunged toward the Master Wizard, only to be caught in the air by his magic strength. Master Wizard struggled as Ukufa's own strength was indeed powerful. So much that he pressed Master Wizard's feet into the ground, cracking the surroundings.

"Allow me to bring some assistance." Obliteran said, holding up fiery hand.

From the ground, bolted up six demons. Snatching away at Ukufa's legs and gnawing at them. The flesh that was present began to be torn apart from his lower body.

"Attack him now!" Master Wizard yelled.

Obliteran struck Ukufa with his aduroblade as Novar followed with his own. Aweran leaped into the air and slashed Ukufa in the chest. They watched as Ukufa fell to the ground. They slowly approached him to see if he was still alive and as they came closer, he rose up from the ground, slashing away at the Master Wizard and Novar. Obliteran sighed.

"Enough of this nonsense." Obliteran said, taking out the Sinthblade. "This shall do the job."

Obliteran prepared to strike Ukufa as more necrofighters were coming toward them. Aweran turned to face them as he grabbed the air and pushed it against them, knocking them back forcefully to the point where they couldn't get back on their feet. Their bones shattered from the impact.

"Move!" Obliteran yelled toward the demons as he struck Ukufa with the Sinthblade in the chest.

In the sky arrived the Emerald Cavaliers. Moving with swiftness to attack the necrofighers with their sharpened crystal swords. Along with them came the Revolter Squadron, settling the aerial battle to a full completion. Ukufa stood on the ground, looking at the Sinthblade in his chest. He chuckled, pulling the blade from his body and tossing it back to Obliteran as he roared.

"How can this be?!" Obliteran questioned.

"I will deal with him." Aweran said, holding his aduroblade steady.

Ukufa prepared to strike Aweran and with one blow as the Master Wizard used his magic once more to trap Ukufa in a frozen state. Aweran took his aduroblade and simply decapitated Ukufa. The undead one's body fell and turned to dust as his necrochete lost its power.

"That's how we deal with them?" Novar said.

"Their leaders it would seem." Aweran answered. "Now, we deal with the Black Hood."

Black Hood was handling Zeena, Ivah, Gaulhan and Savan-Nah easily. His power was beyond theirs in both strength and technicality. With the battleground around them full of dead bodies from all sides. Black Hood knew what was to come as he allowed them all to try and take him down. Everyone made a move and failed. The Ard-Legion went to attack him and he destroyed them and their ships. The Marvels went for a strike, only to be taken down again. The elves attempted to shift Black Hood's mind, yet his mentality was strong for one who was undead. The Emerald Cavaliers flew down toward him and he quickly dealt with them with a energy swipe from his necroblade. Striking even the Revolter Squadron's ark-fighters from the sky. Aweran looked at the battlefield and quickly, he knew his dream was becoming a reality.

"I will not allow it to happen. I won't!"

The remaining necrofighters came to attack once more and in the air, the air itself bolted open, revealing Ocha hovering. The Knights looked, seeing one of their Elders. Ocha looked down toward Aweran and Jad. He nodded as he opened his right hand and exuded energy, destroying the remaining necrofighers with such ease.

"End this now." Ocha said toward Aweran before disappearing.

"A Prophet of The High One." Black Hood said.

Aweran went to strike Black Hood with the staff, Black Hood caught him in his sight and shoved the Knight back.

"No. it will not end this easily."

Aweran arose and held his adorable as the Staff laid on the dirt.

"You want to stop me from causing the future you know? Then fight me. One-on-one. We shall see who comes out to victor."

Aweran caught his breath as he looked around at everyone on the field.

"Everybody. Stand back. This is between me and him."

"Are you sure?" Zeena asked.

"I am. Stand back."

All who remained alive took their steps back as Aweran and Black Hood prepared for a duel. A duel to determine the fate of all life in the Stellarspace.

CHAPTER X

IT CALLS TO HIM

"This is the end." Black Hood grinned, slashing the air with his necroblade.

"You are correct." Aweran said. "This is the end. But not the end you so desire."

Their blades were set, and they each rushed toward each other, clashing the blades to the sound of thunder as the rain started to pour. Everyone moved even further back as Aweran and Black Hood fought. Their blades struck with great blows. Black Hood shoved Aweran, twirling the necroblade as it charged up in power. Aweran noticed the shifting change as he took his aduroblade, deflecting the necroblade, striking the blade as its power bolted from the edge of the blade into the ground. Causing a tremor. Aweran went for more slashes toward Balck Hood as the Undead One dodged the coming atacks. Moving swiftly past them, only inches away from impact. Black Hood raised his right hand, blasting Aweran with a gust of wind.

"How did you do that?" Aweran questioned.

"The Undead have access to all forms of power. It is the living who are limited by this material plane."

Obliteran and Ivah watched on, feeling the Dekar pressing them to enter the fight. They pressed down such dark power to honor the battle. The Magus Court looked on and marveled at Aweran's strength to continue. Whispering under their breaths had Aweran knew the power of magic, he would've defeated Black Hood with ease. The Knights began to cheer Aweran on as he fought back against Black Hood's continued use of the wind.

"Just one strike, my love." Zeena said. "Just one."

Aweran pressed forward through the wind as Black Hood held it steady. Mocking the Knight regarding his faith and source of power. Aweran shook himself, pressing forward with even more strength as his pupils shifted to a golden hue. Aweran stretched his left hand upward, crashing it down into the ground, cracking it for Black Hood's leg to fall into the hole.

"I've had enough of this."

Aweran yelled with a great shout, using the fullness of the Avior to forcefully push Black Hood across the valley, slamming him into the bottom of the mountain. Using the power, Aweran caused the mountain to crash down upon Black Hood, burying him under the massive boulders and sharpened pieces of the mountain. Silence filled the air of the valley.

"Is it over?" Gaulhan asked.

"We're about to find out." Evad pointed toward the downed mountain.

The ground quaked once more. Growing stronger by each tremor. The downed mountain levitated in pieces as Black Hood stood in the midst of it. His energy surged around him as pieces of the mountain levitated in the air around him. His eyes shined brighter for one who has no life in him. Black Hood stretched his arms, tossing the mountain pieces throughout the valley. Everyone else went for cover as the fragments flew past them. Not all were able to find a place of shelter as rain shockers were knocked down. Others impaled by the mountain's shards.

"It seems even your mighty Avior could not end me." Black Hood chuckled. "What will you do, Knight of the Covenant?"

Aweran breathed heavily. Glancing down at his aduroblade. He knew the weapon would not finish the job. So, he sheathed the blade and reached to his back, raising up the Staff of Arkkon. Its shiny presence drew Black Hood toward it. Not out of fear, but curiosity. Black Hood began to walk toward Aweran slowly. Sheathing the necroblade, Black Hood stepped forward with his right arm stretched out. His hand opened. A sign of vulnerability? Or something more?

"Do you know the true nature of a Parcel of Arkkon?"

"I know enough."

"Don't make a mistake, middle one. For if you truly know the power of a Parcel, you would hand it to me and I will do what is right by it."

"You don't know the whole of the future, do you?" Black Hood questioned.

"I know what you do and I will not allow it."

"As I'm sure your Elder had told you, that was only one possible future. It seems you have not seen the future where you kill me and what happens after."

Aweran stood quiet. The Staff ready to be used. His hands tightening the grip. His breath heavily from tiredness.

"What are you talking about?"

"Your dreams told you of my actions and what would do. What I've seen, revealed to me of what you're going to become."

"I have no fear. Speak what you know."

"The future I saw showed me my "death". By your hands. However, due to your enraged spirit, you become endowed with the Dekar. Becoming a Dark Soul. One of the few throughout the annals of the Stellarspace."

"You lie. YOU LIE!"

"I have no purpose to lie. You saw my future. I saw yours. The only question now is… which future is right for the Stellarspace."

"I already made my choice. Regardless of my own selfish reasons."

Black Hood nodded.

"Spoken like a true *Abdhi Knight*."

"Your victory shall not come to pass. Not today. Nor ever."

"Then prove it." Black Hood stopped. "Two paths await you. One, you slay me and stop me from killing your wife and all you care for. But, you become a Dark Soul and you will be an outcast to your family. To your Knights. You will remain to live a life alone. Set to become a nomad, roaming throughout the Stellarspace until the time appointed for your necessary sacrifice or, simply hand me the Parcel of Arkkon, allow as you watch me kill your wife and all those you love and those you do not and rule the Stellarspace for my God of the Dead. However, the choice is yours. ”

Aweran found himself stuck as he looked over to everyone around the battlefield. Their future rested in his hands. His eyes locked onto the Knights. Jad and Amzi stepped forward.

"This is your choice, grandson. I trust you."

"Same here, Aweran. I trust your decision."

Aweran turned, seeing Zeena. She only nodded. He knew her answer. He looked at the Staff and turned his focus toward Black Hood.

"I will not allow my wife or my family to be slaughtered willingly. I will not see the Stellarspace destroyed and all life evaporated so the Dead can dwell in darkness. I will fight as I have this day and the days to come. Today, Black Hood, your death has come."

As Aweran was set to move, he heard the whisper in the wind. Familiar sound. In his mind, he reverted to Thran where he fought Sinth Cain. There, he remembered seeing the shadow figure. Taunting him to embrace the Dekar. Now on Zappdow, the shadow had returned. Standing between him and Black Hood.

"No." Aweran said. "Not again."

Everyone else could only see Aweran talking to himself as it appeared. Yet, Black Hood could see the shadow figure and he grinned.

"What will you do, Knight of the Covenant? What is your decision?"

Aweran tried to shake his mind as an attempt to erase the shadow figure from his sight. But it would not work as the shadow is present on Zappdow with him.

"*Embrace it.*" The Shadow had spoken. "*Embrace the power.*"

"I will not." Aweran replied. "I will make sure life continues to thrive in the Stellarspace. Regardless of my condition."

Black Hood saw as Aweran was talking to the Shadow. Disagreeing with all his energy. Black Hood grew tired of waiting, raising up his necroblade and turning toward Zeena. Aweran saw him as Black Hood winked. Aweran moved forward with the Staff ahead. He screamed with anger as Black Hood swiftly moved to reach Zeena.

"Embrace the Dekar! Embrace it!"

With a loud scream as his pupils shifted from gold to red, the Staff went through the shadow and pressed into Black Hood's chest, impaling him into the remainder of the mountain.

"It is done." The Shadow said, vanishing into smoke.

Aweran looked down, seeing the Staff in Black Hood's chest. The Undead One began to cough off blood as dark as the night sky. through the coughing, he chuckled. Looking Aweran in the eyes, seeing the fiery red present.

"You… made your choice."

"Not for me." Aweran said. "For everyone else. For those who fought and died today and for those who aren't here to fight. I made a selfless decision. I know my choice."

"That you do, Knight of the Covenant. That you…do."

The Undead One had indeed died. His body formed into decayed embers, bellowing through the air of Zappdow. Aweran remained standing as he turned toward everyone else, they saw his beaming eyes. Shining red like Ivah's.

"His eyes." Amzi said.

"No." Jad gasped. "No!"

Aweran looked at everyone. His eyes shifted toward Obliteran and Ivah. He reached down and grabbed his aduroblade. Pointing it toward them.

"Now that the Undead are gone, our war still continues."

"Not today, Knight." Obliteran said, commanding the remaining rainshockers to attack.

The rain shockers fired their ranges toward Aweran. However, the energy remained in the air. Stuck in a frozen state. Aweran held them in place without even lifting a finger. He chuckled before gazing toward them.

"Enough."

The energy bolts returned to the rainshockers, killing them all with headshots. They knew the power of the Avior could to have done so. Obliteran made a run for it to the Sint-Tred. Ivah was intrigued with Aweran's newfound power. In a way, she liked it. Obliterna and Ivah had fled Zappdow. Aweran's new power was the mixed combination of the Avior and the Dekar. The ending solution formed Aweran into a Dark Soul. A powerful being from the legends of the Stellarspace. Aweran stood in place as flames grew around him. Not even the rain could stop the fires. His aduroblade began to warp in colors. From its original dark blue to a fiery red.

"I will make sure the Stellarspace lives. By any means necessary."

The Magus Court had fled. The Ard-Legion, the Novar Force, the remaining Elves, the Sinstorian armies, Savah-Nah and the Marvels had left. Their business concerning the war with Those of Mors was finished. Dovan Pen had disappeared. His ship was gone before the battle was over. Gaulhan had left as a show of respect. He would not fight Aweran. Only the Knights and Evad remained.

"They're lucky I let them leave." Aweran said, pulsing with flames. "Otherwise, this planet would've been their graveyard."

"What do we do?" Amzi asked Jad. "They won't let him back on Helio like this. Look at him. He's consumed with the Dekar."

"I can hear your words, Elder. I am only doing what's best for all life."

"Aweran, grandson. You have the Dekar dwelling within you now. Mixed with the Avior. Such power is forbidden to our laws."

"I know, grandfather. What else was I supposed to do? Let my wife die. Let everyone die."

"No." Zeena said. "We would've found another way."

"There was no other way!"

The air quickened and the ground tremor once more with the thunder and rain. Zeena closed her eyes, raising up her adurostaff.

"I know what I have to do."

"Zeena, what are you doing?" Amzi asked.

"Go to the ships. Prepare for takeoff."

"What are you planning to do?" Jad asked.

"Yeah? What gives?" Evad said.

"I'm going to beat the Dekar out of him."

"Knightess, that is not possible." Jad said. "The only way for him to exult the Dekar is only by him. He must release it."

"I will get him too. Trust me."

They could only stare as she told them to go for the ships. Regretfully, they listened and left. Zeena held the adurostaff forward as Aweran stared at her. While leaving, Jad looked down, seeing the Staff and took it with him.

"What are you doing, my love?" Aweran asked.

"I cannot have the Dekar take you away from me. I will get it out of you."

"You don't understand. I didn't understand. We were taught the Dekar was evil. Malicious. Sinful. But now that I have it in my grasp, its power is incredible. Even with the Avior still in me, I have never felt more powerful. Never."

"Aweran," Zeena said calmly. "the Avior is all you need. It is all you will ever need."

Aweran looked at his left hand, seeing the flames in his palm. The fire red pulsing. He looked to his right hand, holding the now red aduroblade. Hints of blue and gold appeared on the blade. Showcasing the mixture of Avior and Dekar.

"To protect the Stellarspace and all life, it is not enough. With them both, it is enough."

Zeena sighed with a heavy breath.

"Then you leave me no choice."

Atop the mountain range, the Knights and Evad looked on. Zeena rushed toward Aweran with her adurostaff, going for the attack. Aweran blocked it with his aduroblade. Looking her in the eyes, shaking his head.

"Don't do this."

"I have to. You're leaving me no choice."

Zeena went for another strike, this time, awe ran caught the staff in his left hand. The fires overtook half of the adurostaff, burning the blade as its energy evaporated.

"Beloved." Aweran said. "Stop."

"I can't." Zeena said, as tears fell from her eyes. "I can't leave you like this."

Zeena continued to attack Aweran. To the point, his eyes lit up like fire and with a grunting roar, he grabbed her by the throat, slamming her into the ground. Jad went to step forward from the mountain range, only to be held back by Amzi and Evad. Aweran held her down as his aduroblade reached over, raised above her chest.

"Why did you have to keep it going." Aweran said.

"Aweran," Zeena cried. "Please, no. I'm…"

The blade came down as Zeena shouted, "I'm pregnant". The aduroblade paused in the air. Aweran stood confused. Shaking his head. If she was pregnant, she would not have been in the battle. Questing it in his mind, Aweran shook himself. He looked at his burning hands. Thinking. He closed his eyes and opened them. His eyes full of fire as he was able to see through Zeena's body and revealed to himself, she was telling the truth. Aweran stepped back, holding his head, fighting against the Dekar within. Its hold was too powerful to be removed as he screamed in pain of his choice. His screams turned to silence as he stood in the rain. Zeena arose, holding what was left of her adurostaff.

"Aweran?" She said.

"Go." He replied. "Go with the Knights."

"What… what about you?"

"I can't come back with you. The Dekar, I'm too consumed with it. I cannot go back."

Aweran turned to face her. His pupils shifting back and forth between gold and red. Tears fell from them in the same colors.

"Go. Live your life in peace. Take care of our son."

"Son?" Zeena questioned.

"You didn't know yet I see. That's good. You know what to name him."

"I do."

Aweran nodded, turning away.

"Now go."

"I won't stop trying to look for you. I will find a way to set you free."

"I know. I know."

Zeena turned to walk away.

"Zeena." Aweran said. "I love you."

She stood in tears.

"I love you too." She nodded, walking away.

Zeena walked and made it to the Knights and the ships. They looked at her, seeing the tears flowing from her eyes. Jad and Amzi also cried.

70

Even Evad shed a tear as they took off. In a show of kindness, the left one Helio-Sor ship for Aweran as he stood in the valley, covered in the thunderous rainfall. Sheathing his aduroblade. A Dark Soul he had become.

CHAPTER XI

THE DARK SOUL HE WILL BE REMEMBERED

Months have passed since the Battle of Zappdow. The Knights and the Viper Order have returned to their ongoing warfare. The Stellarspace was safe and the nations returned to their previous duties. Treaties were signed. Wars were waged. Conflicts were resolved. Sometime later, Jad took the Staff of Arkkon to Sudravor and given it to the Dwarves for safekeeping as they knew where to hide such a powerful weapon. Jad spoke with Ocha about Aweran sometime later in the armory on Helio. Looking at all the aduroblades from past Knights. Ocha informed him that Aweran had left Zappdow just as they did and went another route.

"Is his still consumed with the Dekar?"

"He is." Ocha said. "It will take some time for him to adjust."

"Is he truly gone from us?"

"There is always a way. Always a chance for redemption. We will not know until it is time."

Nine months later, Zeena was in the countrylands of Coolts as she was in labor. Surrounded by fellow Knights, Evad, handmaidens, and Aweran's mother, Zeena gave birth to a son.

"What will be his name?" Amzi asked.

"Lark. Lark Serkelrod." Zeena nodded, holding her son. "Just as his father wanted."

She looked into baby Lark's eyes, seeing the essence of Aweran within them. A tear fell from her face as she felt a presence around them. Meanwhile, outside of the home. Aweran stood. Cloaked like a shadow in a robe, hooded from being seen. His pupils now violet, a known trait of a Dark Soul. He saw Lark through the window and smiled.

"One day, my son. One day."

Aweran turned and walked away into the vast countrylands to the sunset.

APPENDIX

A look inside the *EverWar Universe.*

ERAS

BoC: *Battle of Caelum*: The calendar era across the Stellarspace.

SPECIES

- **Enash/Enashian:** Man/Woman or Mankind
- Orchs
- Wizards
- Warlocks/Witches
- Elves
- Dwarves
- Gods
- Mechroids

THE FORCES OF THE UNIVERSE

❖ The *Avior*: A spiritual force of energy used by the Abhdi Knights of the Covenant in the universe. The Avior is considered the *"benevolency of the universe"*. Others can tap into the Avior if it makes itself known to them and their willfulness to bond with it. When someone is filled with the Avor, they begin to speak in a tongue unknown to Enash. The abilities of the Avior. The Avior causes the air and the aura to glow a blue, green, gold, or white flame around the user depending on their spirituality and their closeness with the Avior. Those of the Avior uses the phrase, *"Aviorspeed"* when saying goodbye to another. Abilities of the Avior include supernatural strength and agility, spiritual discernment, Healing, Casting out malevolent entities, Loosing holy celestials, Telekinesis, Telepathy, Precognition, Teleportation,

Avior Hedge; which is an invisible, yet powerful and spiritual wall of protection, and the Avior Blast/Bomb; Pressurizing the air into a projectile blast or bomb-like attack.

❖ The *Dekar*: A spiritual force of energy used by the Viper Lords in the universe. The Dekar is considered the *"malevolency of the universe"*. The Dekar feeds on the anger, hatred, envy, jealously, and rage of individuals or groups. The Dekar seduces those who come close to it. The Dekar causes the air and the aura to glow a red, brown, or black flame around the user depending on their spirituality and their closeness with the Dekar. Those of the Dekar are known to say to others *"Submit to the Dekar"* or *"Do as the Dekar wilt"*. Sinth Viper is known as the Dekar physically embodied and is known to be the strongest warrior having the Dekar. Few of the Knights of the Covenant have been given the Dekar. Aweran Serkelrod is known to possess both the Dekar and the Avior as most of the Serkelrod family have dealt with the duel nature of the *Dark Soul*, the combination of both the Avior and Dekar into one being. Abilities of the Dekar include supernatural strength and agility, spiritual discernment, summoning malevolent entities, telekinesis, telepathy, mind control, precognition, teleportation, lust for murder, Dekar Blast/Bomb; Pressurizing the air into a projectile blast or bomb-like attack similar to the Avior, and Dekar Lightning; In which the One of the Dekar is able to project red or black lightning from their hands.

ALLIANCES

• **Knights of the Covenant:** The Abhdi Knights of the Covenant are an order of benevolent, sovereignty, and spiritual group of leaders and warrior knights whom are the main adversary against the Viper Lords. The Knights of the Covenant were created in 21,500 BoC in order to face the Dark Order, ruled by the Viper Lords. Settling on Helio as their main planet, they fought against the Dark Order, later the Viper Order. During the Cavalier Civil

War, the Knights aligned with the Endorians and their king, Siegfried-Ard to combat the Viper Order and their allies. During the War of Helio from 954 BoC to 675 BoC where the Viper Order, Osmanic Empire, Ordowian Wizards, and Sinstorians had made attempts to conquer Helio for themselves. The Knights fought for the protection of their planet and home. In 325 BoC, Helio was sacked by the Viper Order, causing a few of the Knights to flee and recruit help. In turn, they took back Helio and the Abhdi Knights of the Advanced Covenant were created. During the Zorth Wars, Helio was sacked again and left deserted by the Viper Order, which became the Realm of the Viper under the ruler ship of Empress Helvetica and Sinth Viper.

- **Lords of the Viper:** The Viper Lords are an order of malevolent, dictatorial, and sorcery group of leaders who have become the main adversary against the Abhdi Knights of the Covenant and Those of the Avior. Their leaders are called *Sinth*, which means Great Lord in ancient Moralitian. They were created around the aftermath of the Exodus of Sinstor by the Ancient Viper Lords, who later passed down the title to various successors. Many of the Viper Lords went to war against the Abhdi Knights of the Covenant due to the cosmic war of The High One and The Fallen One and the two forces of the Avior and the Dekar. The Viper Lords have also made treaties with other nations such as the Sinstorians and the Crimson Cavalier Force. Since the two have similar interests.

- **Watchmen of Endor:** The guardians of the planet Endor and watchers for the Ard-Kings.

- **Emerald Cavalier Force:** The primary Cavalier Force throughout the Sectors. The Emerald Cavalier became the superpower of the Cavaliers after winning the Cavalier Civil War

- **Marvels of the Universe:** An army of women warriors led by Princess Savan-Nah of Olympya.

- The Warlocks of The West Wind: An elite group of warlocks who guide the patterns of the galaxies.
- Dark Soul: Antiheroes that live amongst the universe that are able to control the *Avior* and the *Dekar*.

- Rainshockers: The imperial army under the control of the Viper.

- Howlshockers: The stealth and aerial military guild.

- Strikefighters: The ranger guild of the sectors.

- Revolter Squadron: The aviation force of the Insurgency.

- Magus Court: The court of wizards led by the Master Wizard.

- Mazoi: The watchers of the Sinstorian grounds under the command of Pharao.

- Venators: A sect of bounty killers who have a hatred for assassins, mercenaries, rangers, strikefighters, and rogue bounty hunters.

CHARACTERS

KNIGHTS OF THE COVENANT/THOSE OF THE AVIOR/HELIOIANS

- ❖ Knight Rayen Grake (743 BoC - 427 BoC): A Knight of the Covenant who lived during the War of Helio. An ancestor to Amzi Grake.

- ❖ Knight Yabel Serkelrod (744 BoC - 430 BoC): A Knight of the Covenant who lived during the War of Helio. An ancestor to Jad Serlekrod, Aweran Serkelrod, and Lark Serkelrod.

- ❖ Knight Iscar Grake (1260 BoC - 530 BoC): An Elder Knight of the Covenant who lived during the War of Helio. An ancestor to Amzi Grake.

❖ **Knight Ocha (N/A):** The ancient Knight of the Covenant who lived during the Cavalier Civil War, War of Helio, and other times before and after.

❖ **Jad Serkelrod (440 BoC -):** The son of Mehar Serkelrod and an Elder Knight of the Covenant. A descendant of Yabel Serkelrod. The father of Laban Serkelrod and grandfather of Aweran Serkelrod, and great-grandfather of Lark Serkelrod.

❖ **Laban Serkelrod (380 BoC - 326 BoC):** The son of Jad Serkelrod and Knight of the Covenant during the Order of the Viper period. Laban was killed when he was defeated by Sinth Tyrannus.

❖ **Amzi Grake (400 BoC -):** A descendant of Rayen Grake and Knight of the Covenant during the siege of Helio and the formation of the Advanced Covenant.

❖ **Ebed El-Ezer (405 BoC -):** A Knight of the Covenant during the siege of Helio and the formation of the Advanced Covenant.

❖ **Novad Tengu (395 BoC -):** A Knight of the Covenant during the siege of Helio and the formation of the Advanced Covenant.

❖ **Orvan Shackleford (395 BoC -):** A Knight of the Covenant during the siege of Helio and the formation of the Advanced Covenant.

❖ **Aweran Serkelrod (349 BoC -):** The son of Laban Serkelrod, granadson of Jad Serkelrod, a Knight of the Covenant, and father of Lark Serkelrod. Aweran later married Zeena and succeeded in ending the Viper Order of Sinth Cain and Sinth Kara before winning the war against the Onyx Cavaliers, ultimately becoming a Dark Soul in the process. Now, a nomad throughout the Stellarspace. Awaiting his final task.

❖ **Zeena Lyh** (346 BoC -): Formerly an unjust prisoner on Area 6776 who aided the Knights of the Covenant to defeat the Viper Order. She later married Aweran Serkelrod and became a Knightess of the Covenant with the formation of the Advanced Covenant. One of the few women to become a member of the Covenant.

❖ **Lark Serkelrod** (265 BoC -): The son of Aweran Serkelrod and Zeena Lyn. Grandson of Laban Serkelrod. Great-grandson of Jad Serkelrod. Descendant of Yabel Serkelrod.

VIPER LORDS/THOSE OF THE DEKAR/MORALTIANS
❖ **Sinth Cain** (349 BoC - 265 BoC): The son of Sinth Zane and Sinth Sahara and the Viper Lord during the War of Helio.

❖ **Sinth Kara** (345 BoC - 265 BoC): The wife of Sinth Cain and Viper Lord during the War of Helio.

❖ **Sinth Obliteran** (356 BoC -): The new Viper Lord during the War against Those of Mors. Succeeding Sinth Cain after his death.

❖ **Sinth Ivah** (346 BoC -): The new Viper Lord during the War against Those of More. Succeeding Sinth Kara after her death.

SINSTORIANS
❖ **Hophra-Apr** (442 BoC -): Pharao of The Late Period.

ELLADIANS

- ❖ **Queen Herena:** The Queen of Ellada. Based in the city of Olympya.

- ❖ **Princess Savan-Nah:** The daughter of Queen Herena and heiress to the Elladian throne.

ENDORIANS

- ❖ **Siegfried-Ard** (1255 BoC - 755 BoC): The legendary Ard-King of Endor, the ancestor of Ansfried-Ard and Eudo-Ard, and the wielder of the Carus Sword. Siegfried came into power after defeating the celestial dragon, Blath the Wicked during the days of the Cavalier Civil War.

- ❖ **Ansfried-Ard** (500 BoC -): The descendant of Siegfried-Ard and the Ard-King of Endor during the War Against Those of Mors.

- ❖ **Eudo-Ard** (367 BoC -): The descendant of Siegfried-Ard and son of Ansfried-Ard. The Ard-Prince of Endor during the War Against Those of Mors.

ORDOWIAN WIZARDS

- ❖ **Master Wizard** (N/A): The legendary and ancient leader of the Magus Court. His will controls all things on the planet Ordow.

- ❖ **Gaulhan The Wizard** (N/A): One of the benevolent wizards on Ordow. An adversary to the Master Wizard and his Magus Court concerning the laws of magic within the universe.

RANGERS/STRIKEFIGHTERS

- ❖ **Evad Nod** (375 BoC -): A skillful ranger within the sectors. He aided Aweran Serkelrod, Zeena Lyh, and the remaining Knights of the Covenant defeat Sinth Cain and Sinth Kara and was of service during the War Against Those of Mors.

BOUNTY HUNTERS/VENATORS

❖ **Dos Ar-Suyaza (3):** The bounty hunter who was hired by the Viper Order to track down the remaining Knights of the Covenant after the Siege of Helio. She is one of the few to wield an adurowhip.

❖ **Jakah Pen:** The Kuwardian Venator and descendant of the House of Pen.

❖ **Dovan Pen:** The son of Jakah Pen and descendant of the House of Pen of Kuward.

DAGOBARIANS

❖ **Thugur Suk:** The leader of the Bloodaxe Clan on the planet Dagobar.

❖ **Thagorth:** The leader of the Cavebone Clan on the planet Dagobar.

ERETSIANS

❖ **King of Iericho:** The king of the city of Iericho.

FAITHS AND RELIGIONS

- **The Ancient/Advanced Covenant:** The faith of the Abhdi and Those of the Avior began with Hevel and Seth and later through the descendants of Sem, mainly through Abraham, his son Yitskhak, and his grandson Ya-Akov. The spread out through the lands of Erets-Alpha before spreading across the universe and ending up on the planet Helio, signalizing the Abhdi a place of dominion. They worship and obey The High One, the One True God and the Creator of the Universe who dwells in the high planet of Caelum. The temple of The High One sits in the city of Tropolton on the planet Helio where the Abhdi and Those of the Avior reside.

- **Worship of the Viper:** The religion of the Viper Order and Those of the Dekar began with Qayin and afterwards the descendants of Kham left Erets-Alpha after a civil war amongst their leader Esav and his twin brother Ya-Akov. They worship a deity who calls himself The Fallen One, a Celestial that rebelled against The High One and began the Battle of Caelum through his rebellion and assembling of other rebellious Celestials. When Esav left Erets-Alpha with his army, he made his way upon the planet of Moraltis where he laid down the foundation for the Viper Order and Those of the Dekar to remain.

- **The Mystical Ones:** The religion of the Dynasties upon the planet of Sinstor. Maintained and controlled through a magocracy, a government dominated by magic and sorcery. A system of polytheistic beliefs and rituals that fill the Sinstorian society. The followers of The Mystical Ones' religion use their abilities of sorcery to give praise to The Mystical Ones in order to help them in battles against other forces. Their leading god is called Xanthou, which is shown through the priests' golden uniforms.

- **Religion of the Dodekatheon:** The religion of the Orosian Empire, Herenian Empire and the Savannian Republic on the planet Ellada. Later ruled by a warrior queen, her princess, and her army of women warriors. Men are viewed as only used for procreation and slavery. Some men are exalted among them for their strengths and honor. The Dodekatheon are a group of twelve to thirteen gods with abilities of their own. They reside on Mount Oros, which stands in the outskirts of Olympya, Ellada's capital city.

- **Regnum Trinitas:** The religion of the Ard family on Endor within their kingdom called Regnum Caelorum after conquering the planet from the Navians. They worship three gods who are later embodied into one body. It is considered blasphemy of Endorians who do not worship the Trinitas.

- **Dagobarism:** The religion of the Orchs and Trolls of Dagobar. The religion favors differently between the clans of Orchs and Trolls throughout the planet. Some worship one god, another three, another twelve, another worship almost an infinite amount of Dagobar gods. They believe barbarism and savagery are the ways of pleasing their gods.

- **The Mining One:** The religion of the Dwarves of Sudravor. They believe in a blacksmith god that assists them with supernatural strengths and endurance to build their weapons and equipment.

- **Ordowian Wizardry:** The religion of the Magus Court on the planet Ordow. They worship The Lord of The Black Arts, who is said to oversee Ordow with an evil eye. Which keeps outsiders at bay from entering the planet.

- **Emerald Cavalier Faith:** The faith of the Emerald Cavalier Force whom obey the rules of the Elders of the Universe. They focus their faith through strength, joy, willpower, endurance, and longsuffering.

WEAPONS

- **Aduroblade:** Aduroblades are the mineral and energy swords used by the Knights of the Covenant, Viper Lords, and many others. The blades are physical replicas of the spiritual aduroblades wielded by the Celestials. The physical replicas were created in 21,500 BoC and given to the Knights of the Covenant and the Viper Lords. Over time, others have built and manufactured their own aduroblades for both good and evil uses. The blades are made of different minerals ranging from planets and sectors such as erets, metal, steel, or titanium. They are covered and coated with star matter and other energetic textures that give the blade its glow and enhanced power. The blades appear in different shapes and sizes. There are straight blades, curved blades, and double blades. The colors of the blades and their aura range from a variety and are chosen to match the characteristics and spirituality of the wielder. The hilts also have their own designs that match the spirituality of the wielder. With the star matter and other energy coating the blade, the blade can cut and pierce through mostly any solid object. Most of the aduroblades are manufactured by the Orchs on Dagobar and the dwarves on Sudravor. Occasionally, they are made on the planet Kingod if there is need for any elemental uses. When two aduroblades clash and are held against each other, they begin to consume the oxygen in the surrounding area. They also give off low-pitched sounds of thunder when clashed. Weapons related to the aduroblade are the aduroaxe, adurostaff, adurowhip, aduroclub, adurohammer, and adurobow.

Wielders of Aduroblades in The Damned Ones

- ❖ Amzi Grake/**Blue**
- ❖ Ebed El-Ezer/**Green**
- ❖ Novad Tengu/**Yellow**
- ❖ Orvan Shackleford/**Orange**
- ❖ Jad Serkelrod/**Gold**
- ❖ Aweran Serkelrod's Aduroblade/**Dark Blue**
- ❖ Zeena Lyh's Adurostaff/**Bright Green**
- ❖ Sinth Cain's Aduroblade/**Dark Red**
- ❖ Sinth Kara's Aduroblade/**Red**
- ❖ Sinth Obliteran's Aduroblade/**Dark Red**
- ❖ Sinth Ivah's Aduroblade/**Red**
- ❖ Black Hood's Necroblade/**Black and White**
- ❖ Ukufa's Necrochete/**Black and White**

- **Sinthblade:** An ancient weapon and first blade of the Viper Lords is an aduroblade of its own. Made of Moraltian granite called brimphur, coated in red star matter, and dipped in the dimensional fire from Abyssus. The blade gives off its own power and a source of heat. Sometimes nearly melting the clothing and material on those not wielding the blade.

Wielders of the Sinthblade in The Damned Ones
- ❖ Sinth Cain
- ❖ Sinth Obliteran

VEHICLES

SHIPS

- **The Attonbitus:** A ship used to travel soldiers and droids to their nearest battlefield.

- **Helio Sor:** The large ship used by the Council of Helio and the Knights of the Ancient Covenant.

- **Sinth-Tred:** The large ship used by the Viper Lords for traveling.

- **Shamhuth:** The destructive ship used by the Onyx Cavalier Force.

- **Perisher:** The star craft of the Onyx Cavalier Force.

- **Strike Rider:** The ship used by Evad Nod.

- **Crusifier:** The ship used by Dovan Pen.

STARFIGHTERS

- **Ark-Fighter:** Commonly used starfighter by the Revolter Squadron.

- **Eglah:** The starfighter ships of the Viper. Piloted by Rainfighters and Aeronauts.

Regnum-Streaker: The starships used by the Ard-Legion.

<u>TERRESTRIAL</u>
- **Land-Veho:** Small, fast transports, similar to pod-like bikes that can hover over land-based areas.

- **Desert-Veho:** Small, fast transports, similar to pod-like bikes that can hover over sand-filled areas.

CREATURES
- **Ard-Hound:** Large species of Dire Wolf that roam the snowy planet of Lithios and the wilderness of Endor.

DEITIES
<u>The Ancient Covenant/The Advanced Covenant</u>
- ❖ **The High One:** Creator and Sovereign Deity of the Universe

<u>Worship of the Viper</u>
- ❖ **The Fallen One:** The Rebellious Celestial Entity

<u>Sinstorian Gods and Goddesses/The Mystical Ones</u>
- ❖ **Aker:** God of Earth and Death
- ❖ **Ammit:** Soul-Eater Goddess
- ❖ **Amonhote, Son of Aph:** Architect, Scribe, Priest, and Public Official
- ❖ **Am-Hah:** Minor God of the Underworld
- ❖ **Amon:** Creator God
- ❖ **Amonet:** Primordial Goddess
- ❖ **Anant:** Goddess of War and Fertility
- ❖ **An-Her:** God of War
- ❖ **Anti:** Falx God
- ❖ **Anapa:** God of Embalming and Protector of the Dead
- ❖ **Anqet:** Goddess of the Yeor Waterlands
- ❖ **Apademak:** Warrior God
- ❖ **Apophis:** God of Chaos

- **Apis:** Oxow God
- **Arenuphis:** Companion Goddess
- **Ahs:** God of Oases
- **Ashtoreth:** Goddess of Fertility, War, and Sexuality
- **Aton:** God Disk of the Sun
- **Atem:** Creator God and God of the Sun
- **Ba'al :** God of the Sky and Storms
- **Baaltis:** Goddess of the City of Gubla
- **Baba:** Papo God of Sexuality and Aggression
- **Banebdjed:** Oxow God
- **Ba-Pef:** Minor God of the Underworld
- **Baaset:** Feline Goddess of Warfare
- **Batt:** Oxow Goddess
- **Benu:** Creator God and God of the Sun
- **Bisu:** Apotropaic God and Protector of Children and Women
- **Bakha:** Oxow God
- **Dedwen:** Incense God
- **Gebeb:** God of the Earth
- **Ha:** God of the Desolates
- **Hapi:** God of the Yeor Flood
- **Hawthor:** Goddess of Joy, Feminine Love, and Motherhood
- **Hatmehyt:** Fish Goddess
- **Hedjedjet:** Skorpio Goddess
- **Hehu:** Personification of Infinity
- **Heka:** Personification of Magic
- **Heget:** Frosc Goddess, Protector of Women in Childbirth
- **Hershef:** Oxow God
- **Heset:** Maternal Oxow Goddess
- **Haru:** God of the Sky and Kingship
- **Hw:** Personification of the Authority of the Spoken Word
- **Iah:** God of the Moon
- **Iatat:** Goddess of Milk and Nursing
- **Ihy:** Child Deity, born to Haru and Hawthor
- **Imentet:** Goddess of the Afterlife
- **Imuthes:** A Sinstorian Polymath of the Third Dynastic Magocracy

- ❖ Istar: Goddess of Fertility, War, and Sexuality. Counterpart of Ashtoreth
- ❖ Iset: Wife of Usiri and Mother of Haru, Goddess of Funerary Rights, Motherhood, Protection, and Magic
- ❖ Iusaas: Primal Goddess
- ❖ Khepra: Solar Creator God
- ❖ Khety: God of the Netherworld
- ❖ Khnemu: Oxow God, Controller of the Yeor Floods
- ❖ Honshu: God of the Moon
- ❖ Mahes: Laon God of War
- ❖ Ma'at: Goddess of Truth, Justice, and Order
- ❖ Maftet: Predatory Goddess
- ❖ Mandui: Lower Solar God
- ❖ Mehyt: Laoness Goddess
- ❖ Menchit: Laoness Goddess of War
- ❖ Mehenet: Serpent God
- ❖ Mehey-Werey: Celestial Oxow Goddess of the Sky
- ❖ Mertseger: Coluber Goddess
- ❖ Meshkent: Goddess of Childbirth
- ❖ Myn: God of Virility
- ❖ Mer-Wer: Oxow God
- ❖ Montju: God of War and the Sun
- ❖ Mout: Consort of Amon
- ❖ Nebethetepet: Goddess Counterpart of Aten
- ❖ Nefer-Temu: God of the Lotus
- ❖ Neheb-Ka: Protective Serpent God
- ❖ Nehmetwy: Minor Goddess
- ❖ Neit: Goddess of War, Hunting, Weaving, and Wisdom
- ❖ Nekhet: Gypture Goddess
- ❖ Nepri: God of Grain
- ❖ Nebthet: Consort
- ❖ Nun: Personification of the Formless
- ❖ Neuth: Goddess of the Sky
- ❖ Pehkhet: Laoness Goddess
- ❖ Pitah: Creator God, God of Craftsmen
- ❖ Qedesh: Goddess of Sexuality and Sacred Ecstasy

- ❖ **Re:** God of the Sun
- ❖ **Raet:** Goddess Counterpart to Re
- ❖ **Renenet:** Goddess of Agriculture
- ❖ **Reshef:** God of War
- ❖ **Renpet:** Goddess of the Year
- ❖ **Satjit:** Goddess of the Southern Regions
- ❖ **Sokar:** Falx God
- ❖ **Sekhet:** Goddess of Fire, War, Dance, Love, and Medicine
- ❖ **Sarapis:** Moraltic/Sinstorian God
- ❖ **Serqet:** Goddess of Skorpios, Medicine, Magic, and Healing
- ❖ **Seskat:** Goddess of Writing and Wisdom
- ❖ **Sutekh:** God of Storms, Desolates, Chaos, and War
- ❖ **Sai:** Personification of Fate
- ❖ **Shed:** Savior God
- ❖ **Shemetet:** Laoness Goddess
- ❖ **Shezmu:** God of Wine and Oil
- ❖ **Shu:** God of the Wind and Air
- ❖ **Sia:** Personification of Perception
- ❖ **Sobki:** God of the Yeor, Army, Military, Fertility, and Dragons
- ❖ **Sopedu:** God of the Sky
- ❖ **Sopet:** Goddess of the Stars
- ❖ **Ta-Bit:** Minor Skorpio Goddess
- ❖ **Ta-Tenen:** Personification of the First Mound of Sinstor
- ❖ **Taueret:** Goddess of Fertility and Childbirth
- ❖ **Tefenet:** Goddess of Moisture
- ❖ **Tetu:** God of the Moon and Knowledge
- ❖ **Tithoes:** Apotropaic God of Tombs, Sleeping, Master of Daemons
- ❖ **Wenut:** Serpent Goddess
- ❖ **Wadjit:** Coluber Goddess
- ❖ **Wadjwir:** God of Fertility
- ❖ **Uneg:** Son of Re, God of the Sky and Death, Maintainer of the Cosmic Order
- ❖ **Wepawet:** Jackal God of War, Victory, Hunting, and Death
- ❖ **Urthekau:** Personification of the Supernatural, Protector of

the Pharao
- ❖ **Wosyet:** Minor Goddess
- ❖ **Yamm:** God of the Sea
- ❖ **Xanthou:** The Supreme Deity of Sinstor, Leader of the Mystical Ones

Religion of the Dodekatheon

- ❖ **Emperor Dyeus:** Elladian God of Thunder and the Sky, Ruler of Mount Oros
- ❖ **Hora-Uno:** Queen of the Elladian Gods and Goddess of Marriage and Family
- ❖ **Posieidawon:** Elladian God of the Seas, Earthquakes, and Tidal Waves
- ❖ **Damater:** Elladian Goddess of Fertility, Agriculture, Nature, and Seasons
- ❖ **Athenai:** Elladian Goddess of Wisdom, War, Science, and Literature
- ❖ **Apellaios:** Elladian God of Light, Prophecy, Inspiration, Poetry, Music, and Art
- ❖ **Artemas:** Elladian Goddess of Hunting, Virginity, Archery, Moon, and Animals
- ❖ **Areios:** Elladian God of War, Violence, and Bloodshed
- ❖ **Aphorodita:** Elladian Goddess of Love, Beauty, and Desire
- ❖ **Haphaistios:** Elladian God of Fire, Master Blacksmith and Craftsmen of the Gods
- ❖ **Hermaion:** Messenger of the Gods, Elladian God of Commerce, Thieves, Eloquence, and Streets
- ❖ **Hestva:** Elladian Goddess of Hearth, Domestication, and Family
- ❖ **Endendros:** Elladian God of Wine, Celebrations, and Ecstasy
- ❖ **Agesilaos:** Elladian God of the Underworld, the Dead, and the Riches under Ellada

Republic Kingdom of Ard
- ❖ All-Father Ard
- ❖ Son-Ard

❖ Spirit of Ard

Sudravorian Gods and Goddesses
   ❖ **The Mining One:** Blacksmith God of the Dwarves

Ordowian Wizardry
   ❖ The Lord of the Black Arts

Emerald Cavalier Faith
   ❖ Elders of the Universe

KEY EVENTS OF THE STELLARSPACE

- **Battle of Caelum (50,000 BoC):** The war between The High One and The Fallen One begins in Caelum after a rebellious act and the release of the Dekar upon the physical universe. Causing a rift throughout the universe and on Erets-Alpha during the first civilization of Enashians. The Battle continues till this day.

- **Great Deluge of Erets-Alpha (15,000 BoC):** Erets-Alpha was filled with evil and corrupted to the point of no fixture. The High One sends a great flood, which kills all life on the planet except for eight enashians who resided in an ark to survive the great waters.

- **Scattering of Enash (14,500 BoC):** The Sons of Noach, Sem, Kham, and Yafet have their children to the point where Erets-Alpha became almost filled with no remaining room and the possibility of an endless war on the planet was inevitable. Therefore, The High One declared to scatter them across the universe. Enashians made their way out into the universe in search for new worlds. Finding many planets with land, nations and cultures began to rise throughout the universe.

- **Cavalier Civil War (1500 BoC):** The cavaliers of the universe wage war against each other over positions of power. The Emerald Cavalier Force and the Crimson Cavalier Force are in a civil war amongst each other, dividing the sectors. Meanwhile, the Knights of the Covenant align with the Endorians to combat the Viper Order. This era was the last sighting of the Onyx Cavaliers before the events of *The Damned Ones*.

- **War of Helio (954-675 BoC):** The Viper Order, The Sinstorians, and The Ordowians agree to take over Helio for its resources and findings on new forms of energy and the potential to use the planet to contact with a more darker force in the universe with the power of the *Dekar* as they battle off against the Knights of the Covenant for dominance over the planet. Knight Rayen defeats the Cavalier of Lithios and searches for Lady Iyera. Yabel combats the Thunder Knight and defeats the Dark Lord of the Shaman. The War of Helio commences with a battle against Empress Venefica with the Ayyubid Dynasty led by Nasir-Ah aligning with the Knights of the Covenant after their takeover of Sinstor.

- **Herenian/Viper War (660 BoC):** Princess Savan-Nah leads the Marvels of the Universe into battle with Princess Chloe, her half-sister. The Covenant Knights and Viper Lords are brought in to join sides.

- **Sacking of Helio (325 BoC):** The Viper Order, after dominating many nations, sack Helio and rid of the Knights of the Covenant.

- **Restoration of Tropolton (325 BoC):** Remaining Knights of the Covenant take the war to the Viper Order with new recruits. They defeat the Viper Lords on the planet Thran to reclaim Helio and the city of Tropolton. From this forms The Advanced Covenant.

- **War Against Those of Mors (265 BoC):** The Covenant/Viper War has risen to the point of total destruction across the universe. The Onyx Cavalier Force appears alongside the Necrofighters. The Wars of Alexondar's successors begins and ends with the takeover of the Viper Order. The Magus Court comes in to assist the sectors from destruction. Aweran Serkelrod gives in to the

Dekar and becomes a Dark Soul, using the forces of the *Avior* and *Dekar* to his own advantage.

WEAPONS

PERSONAL RANGED

- Range - A blaster wielding weapon similar to firearms. Used by Evad Nod.

- Plasma-Range - A blaster wielding weapon that is much more powerful than the Range. Used by Dovan Pen.

SUBSTANCES AND MATERIALS

- **Brimphur:** A burning mineral only found on Moraltis. The mineral was used to forge the Sinthblade.

- **Carusian Ore:** A icy crystal mineral found in the mountains on Endor. The mineral is used as the basis for the Carus Crown and the Carus Sword.

- **Star Matter:** Energy and minerals from the stars of the universe. Commonly used as a coating tool for aduroblades.

- **Calbur/Kuwardian Ore:** A metallic mineral found in distant parts of the planet Kuward. Primarily used as armor for the Kuwardians. It is said to contact mystical properties.

ARTIFACTS

- **Carus Crown:** The royal crown worn by the Ard-Kings of Endor.

- **Parcels of Arkkon:** The Parcels of Arkkon are objects that contain good and evil in many forms. There are known to be many parcels throughout the physical universe. Some contain the knowledge of good and evil. Others possess the power of good and evil. The Parcels of Arkkon entered the physical universe during the *Battle of Caelum* when the Celestials came into the physical plane and scattered the parcels across the universe. The Parcels were once kept protected by The Keepers.

<u>Known Arkkons</u>
- Orbs of Arkkon - Knowledge and Secrets
- Staves of Arkkon - Sovereignty and Dominion
- Trident of Arkkon - Divine Power and Wisdom
- Ankh of Arkkon - Healing and Resurrection
- Swords of Arkkon - Power and Leadership
- Rings of Arkkon - Protection and Offense
- Discs of Arkkon - Holders of Visions
- Minds of Arkkon - Memory and Remembrance
- Amulet of Arkkon - Prophecy and Foresight
- Shrouds of Arkkon - Longevity and Shielding

LANDSCAPE OBJECTS

- **Ziggurat of Urim:** The ancient worship place and temple in the city of Urim.

DOCUMENTS

- **The Book of Ard:** Detailed document of the wars and succession of royalty on the planet of Endor.

- **The Moraltic Bible:** The Laws and Instructions given to the Viper Lords by Sinth Bane after receiving a visitation from The Fallen One during the Cavalier Civil War.

<u>GOVERNMENTS</u>

Caelum Sovereignty
- **Ancient Covenant:** 40,000 BoC - 325 BoC
- **Advanced Covenant:** 325 BoC -

Abyssus Authoritarian
- **Dark Order:** 30,000 BoC - 20,000 BoC
- **Imperium of the Dekar:** 20,000 BoC - 954 BoC
  - **Viperine Empire:** 960 BoC - 673 BoC
- **Viper Order:** 954 BoC - 24 BoC

Eras of Sinstor
- **Early Magocratic Period** - During the Ancient Covenant era
- **Old Kingdom** - During the Imperium of the Dekar era
- **First Dynastic Magocracy** - Beginning of the Cavalier Civil War era
- **Middle Kingdom** - During the Cavalier Civil War era
- **Second Dynastic Magocracy** - The beginning of the War of Helio era
- **Ayyubid Dynasty** - In the middle of the War of Helio era
- **New Kingdom** - During the end of the War of Helio era
- **Third Dynastic Magocracy** - During the Rise of the Supremacy era
- **Mamalik Sultanate** - Towards the end of the Rise of the Supremacy era
- **The Late Period** - During the Order of the Viper era. Current Era.

Eras of Ellada
- Orosian Empire
- Herenian Empire
- Savannian Republic

Eras of Endor
- Kingdom of Ard
- Ard Kingdom of Blath
- Republic Kingdom of Ard

Eras of Utomia
- Utomian Empire
- Navian Republic

Eras of Ordow
- Dystopia of the West Wind
- Order of the Magus Court

DRINKS

- ***Shehar***: A particular beer brewed on Erets-Alpha.

PLANETS

DAGOBAR

THROUGH BRUTALITY AND SHEER AGGRESSION,
DAGOBAR IS THE HOME
PLANET OF THE ORCHS AND TROLLS.
PRIMARILY DOMINATED BY THE
ORCH TRIBES AND THEIR OWN CIVIL WARS, THE TROLLS KEEP THEIR
DISTANCE FROM THE BARBARIC CLASS OF WARRIORS.

EVERWAR
UNIVERSE

ELLADA

ELLADA REMAINS ONE OF THE MOST POWERFUL PLANETS
WITHIN THE STELLARSPACE.
RULED OVER BY QUEEN HERENA,
THE HERENIAN EMPIRE WAS FORMED
AFTER A GREAT WAR.
FROM THERE ARRIVED PRINCESS SAVAN-NAH, WHO LEADS THE PLANET'S ARMY,
THE MARVELS OF THE UNIVERSE
AS THEY GIVE GREAT WORSHIP UNTO MOUNT OROS,
WHERE THE DODEKATHEON, THE GODS OF ELLADA RESIDE.

EVERWAR
UNIVERSE

ENDOR

THE ANCIENT PLANET OF
THE CARUSIAN ORE MINERAL
AND THE KINGDOMS OF
THE ARD DYNASTY.

ENDRO

WHEN MANY NATIONS ACROSS THE STELLARSPACE WERE FORMED, ONE
PLANET WAS DEEMED THE EPICENTER OF A POLITICAL INTERESTS. THIS
PLANET WAS NONE OTHER THAN ENDRO. THE HOME BASE OF THE ORDER
OF COUNCILS. THE MAJOR FIGURES BEHIND ALL POLITICS ACROSS THE
STELLARSPACE TO ENSURE PROTECTION FOR ALL.
EVEN THOUGH MOST OF THE TIME,
THERE ARE OTHERS WHO DISREGARD
THE ENDRO COUNCIL FOR GOOD REASON.

ERETS-ALPHA

THE FIRST AND CENTERPOINT OF THE STELLARSPACE.
THROUGH ITS BEGINNING FIRST WAS PEACE, THEN DESTRUCTION.
AFTERWARDS BEGAN THE WARFARES AND THE CONTENTION.
IT WAS ONLY AFTER THE *DELUGE* AND THE *WAR OF THE SONS* WHEN
THE OTHER PLANETS WERE FORMED AS A MEANS OF PRESERVING
LIFE WITHIN THE STELLARSPACE.
STILL, ERETS-ALPHA IS THE HOME OF MANY ENASHIANS.

EVERWAR UNIVERSE

HELIO

A PLANET NEARLY AS OLD AS THE CREATION OF THE STELLARSPACE.
THIS WORLD HAS BEEN FOUGHT OVER IN COUNTLESS WARS, A
PLANET FILLED WITH VAST MINERALS AND RESOURCES, AN
ABUNDANCE OF GARDENS. THIS PLANET HAD BECAME THE
DWELLING PLACE OF THE OLD COVENANT LEADERS AND
WHERE THE FOUNDATION OF THE
ANCIENT KNIGHTS OF THE COVENANT WERE BORN.

EVERWAR UNIVERSE

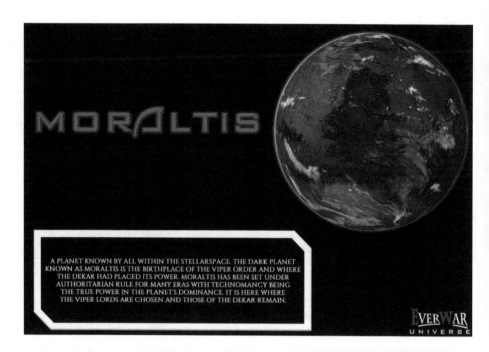

MORALTIS

A PLANET KNOWN BY ALL WITHIN THE STELLARSPACE. THE DARK PLANET
KNOWN AS MORALTIS IS THE BIRTHPLACE OF THE VIPER ORDER AND WHERE
THE DEKAR HAD PLACED ITS POWER. MORALTIS HAS BEEN SET UNDER
AUTHORITARIAN RULE FOR MANY ERAS WITH TECHNOMANCY BEING
THE TRUE POWER IN THE PLANET'S DOMINANCE. IT IS HERE WHERE
THE VIPER LORDS ARE CHOSEN AND THOSE OF THE DEKAR REMAIN.

EVERWAR
UNIVERSE

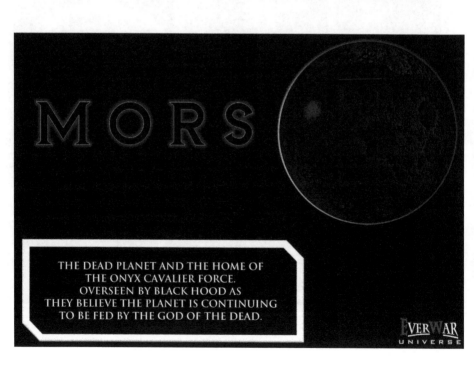

MORS

THE DEAD PLANET AND THE HOME OF
THE ONYX CAVALIER FORCE.
OVERSEEN BY BLACK HOOD AS
THEY BELIEVE THE PLANET IS CONTINUING
TO BE FED BY THE GOD OF THE DEAD.

EVERWAR
UNIVERSE

ORDOW

ORDOW IS THE HOMEWORLD OF SORCERERS AND WITCHES. FROM ITS INCEPTION, ORDOW HELD A PECULIAR POWER WITHIN AND WITH THE MASTER WIZARD'S INTENTIONS, HE HARNESSED THE POWER AND FORMED THE MAGUS COURT, A LEAGUE OF WIZARDS WHO OVERSEE ALL OF ORDOW'S NEEDS AND DESIRES. IT IS SAID WHEN FLYING TOWARD ORDOW, EVEN THE ATMOSPHERE HAS A SPIRIT OF ITS OWN.

EVERWAR
UNIVERSE

R O

THE BURNING PLANET WITHIN THE STELLARSPACE. A PLANET OVERTAKEN BY MASSIVE VOLCANOES AND RIVERS OF FLOWING LAVA.

EVERWAR
UNIVERSE

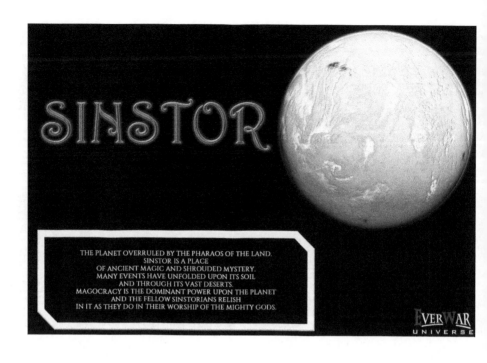

SINSTOR

THE PLANET OVERRULED BY THE PHARAOS OF THE LAND.
SINSTOR IS A PLACE
OF ANCIENT MAGIC AND SHROUDED MYSTERY.
MANY EVENTS HAVE UNFOLDED UPON ITS SOIL
AND THROUGH ITS VAST DESERTS.
MAGOCRACY IS THE DOMINANT POWER UPON THE PLANET
AND THE FELLOW SINSTORIANS RELISH
IN IT AS THEY DO IN THEIR WORSHIP OF THE MIGHTY GODS.

EVERWAR
UNIVERSE

THRAN

THE PLANET WHERE BATTLES ARE FOUGHT AND WARS END. THRAN IS A
CONSTANT BATTLEGROUND FOR ALL NATIONS THROUGHOUT THE
STELLARSPACE. IT IS THE PLACE WHERE MANY CONFLICTS COME TO AN END.
ALTHOUGH, MANY ARE NOT FAMILIAR WITH THE LEGEND OF THE THRAN
BEAST, THE POWERFUL SEA DRAGON WHICH DWELLS UNDER THRAN'S DARK
WATERS.

EVERWAR
UNIVERSE

UTOMIA

THE STARRY AND WONDER PLANET.
RULED BY THE NAVIAN EMPIRE. FORMERLY
KNOWN AS THE UTOMIAN REPUBLIC.
A PLANET FULL OF A THRIVING SOCIETY.

EVER**WAR**
UNIVERSE

ZAPPDOW

A PECULIAR PLANET WITHIN THE STELLARSPACE.
KNOWN FOR ITS CONSTANT THUNDERSTORMS
AND IMMENSE HEAT.

EVER**WAR**
UNIVERSE

CONCEPT ART

ADUROBLADE CONCEPT

SINTHBLADE CONCEPT

WITH THE PROSE SERIES OFFICIALLY OVER. (*UNLESS SOMEONE COMES ALONG WITH A STORY WORTH TELLING IN THE FUTURE..*) THE *EVERWAR UNIVERSE* WILL CONTINUE ON THROUGH ANIMATION, VIDEO GAMES, TV, FILM, AND ATTRACTIONS.

TRANSMEDIA STORYELLING IS THE FUTURE OF THE STELLARSPACE.

- *Ty'Ron W. C. Robinson II – Creator/Author*

ABOUT THE AUTHOR

Ty'Ron W. C. Robinson II is the owner of The Dark Titan Company and the creator/author of several works of fiction. Including the *Dark Titan Universe Saga*, The Haunted City Saga, EverWar Universe, Symbolum Venatores, and more.

More information pertaining to the author and stories can be found at thedarktitancompany.com, darktitanentertainment.com, and darktitanpublishing.com.

FOLLOW THE UNIVERSE OF REALMS

Twitter: @DarkTitanBooks

Instagram: @darktitanbooks

Minds: @darktitanentertainment

YouTube: @DarkTitan

TikTok: @thedarktitancompany

Milton Keynes UK
Ingram Content Group UK Ltd.
UKHW022036081123
432235UK00016B/203/J